Laughton Osborn

Bianca Capello

A tragedy

Laughton Osborn

Bianca Capello
A tragedy

ISBN/EAN: 9783337721930

Printed in Europe, USA, Canada, Australia, Japan

Cover: Foto ©Andreas Hilbeck / pixelio.de

More available books at **www.hansebooks.com**

BIANCA CAPELLO

A TRAGEDY

BEING IN COMPLETION OF THE
FIRST VOLUME OF THE DRAMATIC SERIES

BY

LAUGHTON OSBORN

NEW YORK
J A M E S   M I L L E R
647 BROADWAY
1868

BIANCA CAPELLO

MDCCCLV

CHARACTERS

Primary

FRANCESCO-MARIA DE' MEDICI, *Grand Duke of Tuscany.*

CARDINAL FERDINANDO DE' MEDICI, } *his brothers.*
DON PIETRO DE' MEDICI,

MALOCUORE, *a Gentleman of the Grand-duke's household, and his confidant.*

PIETRO BONAVENTURI, *at first a Clerk in the banking-house of Salviati in Venice, but subsequently the Grand-duke's Favorite and Intendant.*

LUCA SENNUCCIO, *his fellow-clerk and friend, and subsequently of the G. Duke's household.*

CARLO ANTONIO DEL POZZO, *Arch-* ⎫
bishop of Pisa, — at one time ⎪
Auditor of the Treasury, ⎬ *both of the*
OTTAVIO ABBIOSO, *Coadjutor-Bish-* ⎪ *Grand-duke's Cabinet.*
op of Pistoia and Florentine ⎪
Secretary at Venice, ⎭

BIANCA CAPELLO, *at first wife of Bonaventuri, subsequently Grand Duchess of Tuscany.*

DONNA ISABELLA DE' MEDICI, *the Grand-duke's sister.*

SIGNORA MALOCUORE, *wife of Malocuore.*

Secondary

PAOLO GIORDANO ORSINI, *Duke of Bracciano, husband of Isabella de' Medici.*

BARTOLOMMEO CAPELLO, *Senator of Venice, Bianca's father.*

VITTORIO CAPELLO, *her brother.*

GRIMANI, *Patriarch of Aquileia, her uncle.*

204

TIEPOLO, } *Venetian Senators, special Ambassadors from the*
MICHIELI, } *Republic.*

BACCIO BALDINI, }
PIETRO CAPPELLI, } *Court Physicians.*

SCHERANO, }
MASNADIERE, }
MALANDRINO, } *assassins.*
SGHERRO, }

CAGNOTTO, }
BRENNA, } *armed servants of the Favorite.*

DONNA ELEONORA DI TOLEDO, *wife of Don Pietro.*
DONNA VIRGINIA DE' MEDICI, *the Grand-duke's half-sister,*
betrothed and subsequently married to Don Cesare d' Este
Bonaventuri's MOTHER.
AIA, *Bianca's Governess.*
Count Ulisse Bentivoglio. *A Page in Bonaventuri's*
household. Two Assassins.

Mute Persons

PELLEGRINA, *Bianca's Daughter, wife of Bentivoglio.* DON CE-
SARE D' ESTE. *Senators. Magistrates. Lords and*
Ladies of the Court. Venetian Nobles.
Pages. Soldiers. Servants.

SCENE. *In the First Act, in Venice; in a portion of the Fourth,*
in Rome; for the rest of the play, in Florence, until
the catastrophe, — which takes place at Caiano,
in the neighborhood of Florence.
COSTUMES. *Those of the latter half of the 16th Century.*

BIANCA CAPELLO

ACT THE FIRST

*Scene I. A room in the Apartment of Bonaventuri
in the Casa Salviati in Venice.*

BONAVENTURI. SENNUCCIO.

Senn. Capello's daughter? Thou art doubly mad!
Bonav. All passion is but madness. Why not mine?
Senn. All passion is not madness — not as thine.
   Thou art in impulse, act, and object mad.
   To love the flower of all Venetian maids,
   That was not sane: why! art thou not, as I,
   But Salviati's servant, and low-born? —
Bonav. What has? ——
          Senn. To dare to make thy passion known,
   That was still madder. —
             Bonav. Could I will it else?

Can ? ——

Senn. But to seek —— What dost thou seek in fine ?

Bonav. Nothing. Wilt hear me speak ? Thou art no more
　Luke my companion, friendly although rough,
　And counseling like an elder brother ; thou
　Speak'st without pity, hast no sympathy,
　Though 't was for that, and through the show of that
　Alone, I utter'd what no human ear
　Should otherwise have learn'd. Thou did'st seduce me
　By thy great urgence and thy tone of love
　To throw myself upon thy offer'd breast,
　And then brok'st from me, with a shout and laugh.

Senn. A shout, Pietro¹, if thou so must phrase it,
　For I was sore amaz'd ;. but not a laugh.

Bonav. Yes, with a laugh. For what is it but scorn
　That makes thee treat my passion as insane ?
　I look'd for sober counsel, — for reproof ;
　But yet for pity, — not for mockery.

　　　　　　　　　　　Senn. No.

Nor hadst it. Canst thou not allowance make
For my surprise ? It seem'd so strange a thing,
When I beheld thee pining and cast down,
Thy sparkling eyes grown heavy like a girl's
Sick of her maidhood, and thy jocund laugh,
That had at times contagion even for me,
Turn'd to a melancholy vacant smile,
As if thy soul were in the topmost clouds,
And oft in answer to my happiest speech
Heard thy inapplicable words, or met,
As often quite, thy start, and stare, and " Luke,

Forgive me! Do not think me rude! I am
Scarce well": it seem'd so strange a thing,
To learn at last thou wast heart-sick for one
So high above thee, and so rarely bright,
It was as though thou sighedst for the moon.—
Bonav. Endymion did.
     Senn. That was in fable.
        Bonav. Not
In fable though, the Moon return'd his sighs.
That was the natural sequel of true passion,
Which fires in turn.
    Senn. Thou hast the fable wrong.
It was the Moon lov'd him, who slept through all.
Thou may'st be handsome as the Latmian boy.
Like him, thy moon consoles thee but in dreams.
Bonav. Not so, by Heaven! for I am wide awake,
And —— [*checking himself.*]
Senn. Darest not say, that thou art lov'd in turn?
Bonav. I dare not say it, but ——
    . *Senn.* Thou look'st it! Now,
This is sheer lunacy! Moonstruck Pietro!
Art thou then well awake?
      Bonav. I am awake:
Awake to find that I have dream'd of things
Not less unreal than Diana's kisses;
As of thy heart for instance, and the place
Methought I held in it; awake to learn,
And learn to my dismay, that souls as calm
And as profound as thine may stir with envy.

Senn. Pietro! — But so be it. It is well
That I should read my nature. It may be
That thou divinest right. Our friend's self-love
Jars harshly on the quick sense of our own.
'T is Heaven's foresight. — But, if envy's gust
Ruffle the surface of my graver spirit,
Thy vain presumption surges fathom-deep.

Bonav. Vain? and presumption? It is kindly said!

Senn. 'T is said, at least, in no disdain of thee.
Capello's blood flows from the mountain rill;
Thine is like mine, the puddle: so men think.

Senn. But what of these distinctions knows the heart,
Or asks? Love is no herald; flesh and blood,
Not gules and argent, are his lore: nor can
The Doge's bonnet, did its jewel'd band
Gleam on Capello's haughty forehead, throw
The terror of his function round his child.
She is herself alone; lov'd for herself.

Senn. 'T is thus thine eyes behold her. But for hers ——

Bonav. They look not through her father's robe of state.
Besides, I am not sure Bianca knows ——

Senn. Bianca? Really! ——

            Bonav. Wherefore not? I would
I had not so betray'd me! But thus far
Since thou hast brought me to confess, hear on.
Hear on? No! read! Read there!

Handing a note to SENNUCCIO, *after kissing it with rapture.*
   Then, eagerly watching his countenance as he reads,
     BONAVENTURI *continues triumphantly:*

Art dumb? Is that
Diana's beam? And am I yet asleep?

Senn. I see no signature — no name without.
Comes this indeed from her? from her to thee?

Bonav. To me from her.

Senn. It passes all belief!
Is there no fraud? Women have snar'd ere now.
What means this mystery? [*indicating a place
on the note.*

Bonav. First give it voice. Read out.
Let my ears drink the rapture that my eyes
Have ten times in the hour past reel'd with; let
My heart renew its triumph. Read! Read all!

Senn. [*reading.*
" Surprise — I would not say distrust or fear —
Made me, perchance, seem harsher than I meant.
I would amend my fault, if one have been.
Does thy petition, in thy friend's behoof,
Bear to be urg'd again, so let me hear it:
That with prepared ears I may decide,
If with my quality and maiden shame
It suit to grant it. She who bears thee this
Will tell thee more. Thou mayst confide in her,
As I do in thy nobleness." — And —— Well?

Bonav. Wilt thou without rude hindrance hear me through?

SENNUCCIO *nods gravely.*

Resolv'd to speak or die, I chose an hour
When Blanche's governess came from her prayers,
And told her that a case of life and death

Depended on the favor of her ward;
Whose intercession in a friend's behalf
I must implore in person. The good dame,
By my strong urgence mov'd — how could she else ?
I pray'd as to a saint, — at last consented
That on the morrow I should be receiv'd
Into their barge, and to her lady's ear
Breathe out my supplication.
                    Senn. And thou went'st?
Pietro! ——
Bonav. Hush! — I went. Bianca's hand —
'T could be no other there, so small, so white!
From the Capello's gondol-window wav'd
A kerchief. 'T was a minute. In the next,
I stood before her — knelt. Her veil was dropp'd,
Even as I entered, by her guardian's hand.
Senn. 'T was well the hag had some small conscience.
                    Bonav. Luke! ——
At my mute look and motion of reserve,
Bianca made the dame some steps retire,
Then softly bade me rise and speak.² O me !
The voice took from me all my power. Perhaps
The innocent young creature redd the cause
Of my fresh agitation, if already
Looks, gesture, attitude had not betray'd
My soul's true object; for her own sweet speech
Trembled a little, as, with downcast mien,
She bade me gain composure, and once more
Enjoin'd me rise, if I would have her hear.

My thoughts came back. I told her the deceit
My friend's despairing passion made me practice ;
That not upon her father's lips, but hers,
Hung the decision of his fate; and then,
When I had pour'd forth all my passionate thoughts,
Which no more broke in the utterance, but rush'd
One rapid torrent, of such musical flow
That my own senses vibrated, and love
Took from the echo of itself new force, —
Then did I pray that I might see the face
That had wrought such sweet mischief. She complied.
O Luke! ——

  Senn. Take breath, Endymion.

     Bonav. Would'st thou hear ?

Senn. Ay ! But expect no sympathy.

     Bonav. Not now.

I end the tale but to excuse myself. —
Transported, madden'd if thou will, by charms
Which gained by nearness, and which pudency
Color'd to make transcendent, I avow'd
My friend and I were one. And now in haste
Comes up the governess, and with reproaches
Lets down her lady's veil and bids me go.
I rose — for still I had knelt. "And shall my friend,''
I ask'd, "dare then to hope? " — "Hope all men may,'
Bianca said : " They who are right, hope always."

Senn. A most sententious maiden ! — Well, so far,
The mystery is solv'd. But this remains.
Think'st thou the lady knows thee not her peer ?

She writes, " Thy nobleness." What means that phrase ?
Bonav. For one so patient, thou art much in haste.
Give me the note. — Thou hast heard I left abruptly.
I fear, alas ! she knows not what I am. [*with dejection.*
Senn. Fear, say'st thou ?   By St. Luke! 'tis nobly said !
I too did fear, Pietro. [*extending his hand, which Bona-
venturi does not touch.*
   Bonav. [*haughtily.*] What then ?
                  Senn. This:
Thy honorable nature had succumb'd.
No! [*as Bonav. is going.*
   in this mood thou leav'st me not.
   Bonav. [*endeavoring to free himself.*] Why stay,
When from thy coldness and distrustful thoughts
I fly to Paradise ? and not to play
The Serpent, as thou ——
         Senn. As I do not think.
Thou shalt stay till thou hear'st me ; for 'tis thou
That wrong'st me, not I thee.   Do I not know thee?
Daring, impetuous, yet of kindly heart,
Who among men hath honor, if not thou ?
But what is human honor ?   This one thinks,
Not for wide worlds he would commit a theft,
Yet plots, cabals, o'erreaches, undermines,
And calls it policy.   This, who the rare
And precious gift enjoys to never lie,
Save in surprise or fright of shame, belies
His conscience daily by complaisant smiles,
And in the exaction of his self-love feigns

Desires he feels not! Affluence clips the wings
Of honesty, which flies distress;[3] and longing
Indulg'd melts virtue that was cold as snow.
Thou art as open as the broad sun-light,
And all a man; yet what ensures thy soul,
When passion makes it agony to part,
And happiness, and pride, and dread of shame,
And pity itself, all urge thee to defer?

Bonav. My present action. She who brought this billet —
Given me this morn at mass — a fortnight gone
Since in the gondola I knelt and sigh'd —
Comes at the night's fifth hour — 'tis now at hand —

                     [*looking off the scene.*

To lead me to Bianca — to her home.

Senn. At the Capello's palace?

                 Bonav. At the palace.

Senn. Whither thou goest, to? ——

                 Bonav. Tell Bianca all:
To end the dream which laps, perhaps, her senses,
But is no dream for mine.

                 Senn. This thou wilt do?

Bonav. I will. [*with dejection, yet firmly.*

Senn. Now Heaven make thee blest, Pietro!
Happen what may, thou 'lt bear no self-reproach
On the charg'd conscience. Yet, ah be advis'd!
Subdue this love? To what end can it lead?
Know'st thou not Venice and the dreaded Ten?
Let but her sire denounce thee to the Signory,
Thy life is not a summer's day.

Bonav. So be it.

Clock within strikes Five.

Hark, from the clock-tower! [*Exit precipitately.*

         Senn. Rash, but gallant heart!

Thou goest downright to manifest destruction:

For my cold counsel tempers not thy pulse.

Thou hast call'd it envy. Envy! Can it be?

So. Let me sift myself. I would not make

One of another class with those I sketch'd;

Men who sin not themselves, nor play the fool,

But grudge the mirth and joy of those who do.

            [*Exit — thoughtfully.*

Scene II.

In the Casa Capello. A room in Bianca's Apartment.

Bianca *and the* Governess.

*Bianca walking up and down in agitation. She stops to
look off the scene.*

Gov. 'T is but two minutes. Think!
                    Bian. 'T is but the street
Between us. Two are twice too much. Were I
As he, I should not be so long. And yet
          She ceases to address her attendant.
How ardent was he! Had he not been so,
I had not ventur'd. But what will he think?
Gov. What matters? He is noble; then, must see
How you have suffer'd.
                    Bian. Yes, could he but know
That for the last ten days I scarce have slept,
Fearing a thousand things, and hoping more ——
Why came he not to the house? He must have seen
How well he pleas'd me. Could he else, so made?
Gov. That may you say. And such a generous hand!
Pure, all pure gold, the purse he gave me leaving.
It is a right rich house.
                    Bian. Four minutes more!

O he is laggard! Hark but! —— On the stair!
Now! — Now! — The door, good nurse!

Enter BONAVENTURI.

BIANCA *runs up, as if to throw herself into his arms, but
stops, sinks on a seat, and extends her hand, which* BONA-
VENTURI, *kneeling, takes and kisses.*

        Bonav. O gentle lady! —
 Dare I once more? —— 'T is what I scarce had
  hoped !
Bian. You speak to chide me. Have I been too bold ?
Bonav. Bold ? 'T was an angel's impulse ! But for this,
 How could I, so unworthy, dare again ? —
 I could but silent suffer, as till now,
 Through the long weary fortnight, since the hour
 I knelt and ventur'd in another's name
 To tell you I ador'd you, I have suffer'd.
 But this one minute, were it now to end,
 Repays me, O for all! for all! [*kissing tenderly and
        rapturously her hand.*
      Bian. Alas!
 And I —— But rise. [*withdrawing gently her hand.*
       — I fear'd —— I know not well
 What 't was I fear'd. Is it, I was unkind ?
 I would not be, believe me. If in error,
 In the surprise, the —— if I said too little,
 Or, O! too much, forgive me, and forget
 All that is wrong in what I said or wrote,

For it has much annoy'd me.

Bonav. This for me ?
I have not merited that thou shouldst lose
One half-hour's rest, shouldst feel one moment's care,
For such as I. Forgiveness? Let me pray,
Once more upon my knees, to be forgiven
For the deceit through which this hour is mine.
Thou smilest. Best, as brightest of thy sex!
Hast thou been conscious of my long, long love,
And find'st it not so criminal? Indeed,
I could no longer bear it; I had died,
Had I not spoken. [*He takes her hand. Bianca, in*
her reply, folds the other over his.

Bian. Wherefore died? Seem'd then
Bianca so ungentle, when thine eyes
From thy sad window watch'd her going out,
And waited her return? Didst thou not think,
Vain man! the eloquence of those wistful looks
Made echoes sometimes in the maiden heart
That knew as yet no love but that of friends
And parents? Henceforth thou wilt not despond?
Thou hast stolen an easy way to Blanche's heart!
Live then to guard it; live for *her*, live *with* her.

Bonav. Forever! O such life were one long dream
Of Paradise, with no forbidden fruit,
No serpent, and no —— Must I not despond?
The dream already breaks; the cherub stands
Before the portal with the flaming sword,
And Heaven's decree admits of no reversal.

Bian. What mean'st thou?

    Bonav. Can this night endure forever?
Wouldst thou permit, or could I dare request
Again admittance to thy chamber?

        Bian. No!
Why shouldst thou need? My father ——

         Bonav. O my God!

  Springing up, he comes forward, and BIANCA *follows him to the front of the scene.*

  The GOVERNESS *also comes nearer, though keeping still in the background.*

Bian. What is it ails thee? In my father's name
Should be no terror. Thou art not his foe?

Bonav. O no! But in thy father's blood is that,
Though both are mortal, will not mix with mine.

Bian. Yet thou art noble ——.

      Bonav. Noble?

        Bian. And thy house
Is one whose stem might be entwin'd with ours.

Bonav. My house? Whom tak'st thou me for?— O my
fears!

Bian. Wo 's me!—Art thou not Salviati?

        Bonav. No!

Bian. Nor of his kin?

    Bonav. Alas! nor of his kin.

Bian. O Heaven!— Speak out! Thou would'st not torture me
Who have been kind to thee? Say what thou art.

Bonav. Bonaventuri, Salviati's clerk.

BIANCA *sinks on a chair, which the* GOVERNESS
has brought her, and covers her face with both hands.
BONAVENTURI *kneels softly before her.*
Oh dearest lady! whom I have so wrong'd
Not of my will, think not too hardly of me!
Not by surprise, not from reluctant lips
This truth was wrung; believe me, O believe!
I fear'd your error, and I came to tell,
To tell you all. Do not be angry with me!
Bonav. Alas! I have no anger, only sorrow,
Sorrow for both of us. — [*She drops her hands.*
— Bonaventuri! —

[*with a faint smile.*
Thou seest I fear not to pronounce thy name —
What I have said can never be recall'd;
What I have done, that will not be forgotten :
If it will soothe thy anguish at this parting,
To know I share it, be it even so.
And now — farewell! [*extending her hand.*
Bonav. Not yet! In pity, no!
Thou canst not so dismiss me! Think, O think,
Of the long hours where hope shall never more,
Never, make day for me! Think of the past,
The month on month my yearning heart hath hunger'd,
Feeding itself upon the single thought
Of such an hour as this, which thou wouldst shorten
Thou dost not seem to scorn me: let me then
Lie at thy feet, and, for some minutes still,
Dream I 'm in Heaven.

Bian. To awaken where?
Since part we must, why struggle to obtain
A respite that at best can be but brief?

Bonav. Because it is my life, and all beyond
Is death and darkness.

              Bian. Hast thou then for me
No thought? Canst thou bear nought for my sake?

              Bonav. [*rising quickly.*] Yes;
An age of heartache, will it give you ease.
I was but selfish: I will go. I go. [*moving sadly away,*
             with his eyes still on Bianca, who rises.
Gov. [*laying her hand on Bonaventuri's arm.*
Come then, young man, since you are no one now.
It is high time that you were gone.

              Bian. How now!
Aia, know better thine own place, and mine;
And, where I honor, learn to show at least
Some sign of reverence.

       Gov. [*low, to herself.*] What a change is here!
She was a child this morning!

              Bian. Mind her not:
I am the mistress here. — Look not so mournful!
             [*giving her hand.*
And yet I cannot bid thee not remember.

Bonav. Could I obey? — Wilt thou remember me?
Wilt thou mourn for me, if—— Bianca! (so —
Permit me — 't is the only time — to call thee)
Whatever happen, thou wilt not condemn me?
Thou wilt not mix my errors with my birth,

And deem me all unworthy?

    Bian. Seem I such?
What mean'st thou?

   Bonav. Heaven bless thee! and — Farewell!
As he is going, BIANCA, *who has seemed a moment*
 stupefied, suddenly hastens to him.
Bian. Bonaventuri!

   Bonav. Why command me back?
I thought it past.

   Bian. [*taking his hand, looks fixedly and anx-*
iously in his face.] What didst thou mean by that?
There is a desperation in thy look
That should not be there. Art thou not a man?
Is love the only object of man's being?
There be far nobler aims; and thou art young,
Ardent, and bold. Live that I may not blush
To have shown thee favor, live because thou hast
Thy life thou knowest not why, and hast no right
To squander it as if it were thy choice.
More, thou didst lay it at my feet: 't is mine,
If thou concede it not, as fits thee rather,
Thy country's, and thy fellow-men's, thy God's!
Why art thou silent? Why that stony look
Of passionless despair? Thou dost not love me!
Thou wouldst not else ——

   Bonav. Bianca! [*slowly.*

    Bian. Promise then
Thou wilt do nothing desperate, thou wilt
Do nothing till thou hear'st from me. Thou canst

Never more enter here ——

      Gov. [*who has looked on Bianca all the while with amazement.*] Not by my will!

Bian. Aia!— But thou shalt hear from me, thou wilt
Write to me by the messenger, and send.
Dost thou then promise — solemnly ?

      Bonav. I do —
By all God's holy angels! — thou art one.

Bian. Stoop! — With this kiss [*kissing him solemnly on the forehead.*
      thou hast Bianca's — friendship.
I vow it — hear, Heaven! So long as thou do nought
To forfeit it. Now go at once; go quickly.
The Mooress waits without to lead thee down.

BONAVENTURI *kissing passionately* BIANCA'S *hand, presses it, clasped, a moment to his heart, then moves to the door, his face still turned on* BIANCA.

Gov. [*as she conducts him out.*
      Mary be prais'd! here never to come more.

      [*Exeunt Bonav. and Gov.*

BIANCA *gazes a moment fixedly on the door, then wrings her hands in a paroxysm of grief.*

Bian. Now he is gone, I am a child again.
O Mary Mother! St. Mark! and gentle Luke! [*kneeling.*
All angels and good saints! pray, pray for me!
Aid me against myself; I have no strength
To make the sacrifice which Heaven commands.

She buries her face in the cushion of the chair, sobbing bitterly. — Scene closes.

SCENE III.

A room in Sennuccio's apartment, in the Casa Salviati.
SENNUCCIO *sitting at a table reading.*

Enter BONAVENTURI.

SENNUCCIO *looks up, then resumes his occupation.*
BONAVENTURI *looks at him for some moments, then lays
before him an open letter.*

Bonav. Read.
  Senn. From Bianca? [*looking at the signature.*
    Bonav. Ay.   But read aloud.
Senn. [*reading.*
 " Thou ask'st in vain. There are no means. Not one.
My governess is proof to prayers and gold.
She threatens even, if I give not o'er,
To expose us to my father.   What to do?
I am so watch'd, by day as well as night,
I cannot meet thee elsewhere, and here now
Would put thy life in peril and my fame.
Write me no more such letters, O in pity!
They burn into my brain.   My nights are frightful;
And from brief slumbers and distracting dreams
I wake to weep, to ponder our sad lot,
To see perhaps thy wan face at the casement,

Think on thy anguish, which redoubles mine,
And deem sometimes 't were better both were dead.
I thought myself more strong when thou wast by,
But in thy absence find myself the weaker.
Have then, I pray, compassion on us both."
Thou wilt have, wilt thou not ?

                 Bonav. It is too late.
I have already written, three days since.
Senn. And was that generous ?

                 Bonav. It was simply just.
I had compassion on herself and me.
Senn. Explain.

       Bonav. For that I come ; and for thy aid. —
I wrote to say, I would receive her here,
Here in my rooms, in Salviati's house.
Senn. [*starting up. They both come forward.*
    Art thou distracted ?

               Bonav. Desperate alone.
I never spoke more sanely in my life.
My plan is for salvation. [*Senn. about to interrupt.*
                 Hear ! then judge.
I told her I would watch for three whole nights,
Until the day broke. Coming, she should be
Sacred before me as an enshrin'd saint
Before its votary. This I truly vow'd,
By her dead mother, by her living self.
But coming not, I cast off hope forever,
And with it my young life, then nothing worth.
Two nights have pass'd in vain. This early morn

I saw her at a window. O so white!
So suppliant with those melancholy eyes!
Whose deep-sunk and impurpled orbits show'd
Long watching, passion, and the pine of care, —
That my fast purpose trembled. But it holds.
The third night comes : and with it — comes Bianca.
I feel it in my soul.

    Senn. Thou tak'st her for?——

Bonav. Capello's child, high-thoughted and most pure ;
 Yet a deep-loving woman. She will trust me.
Senn. And thou?

   Bonav. Will keep my oath. I swear it here,
As I have sworn it on my knees to God.
Witness ye saints! my sister, now in Heaven,
Would not be more immaculate by me
Than she shall be this night!

    Senn. What then your aim?

Bonav. To marry her. Thou 'lt aid me ?

      Senn. No!

       Bonav. Thou wilt.
Thou wouldst not scruple to give life to both.
Senn. Ay, must I do it wrongly. But this life ! ·
To take her from the lap of luxury, to expose her,
This delicate child, soft-nurtur'd, and high-plac'd,
This daintiest flower of all Venetian land,
To the bleak winds of penury, transplanted
To an ungenial and a barren soil :

   Bonaventuri *walks about impatiently.*

Is this — Stop! listen to me!— this your life ?

Better to slay her outright, and to die for 't!
That were a crime, but 't would be truer mercy.
But this is idle talk: for, say she come,
How know'st thou she is reckless as thyself?
'T is a long leap, a marriage!
     Bonav. She will take it,
When there is no way left her but to leap.
Senn. Ha!
 Bonav. Wilt thou aid me, Luca? 'T is not much.
Senn. Let me hear further.
    Bonav. When Bianca comes,
She leaves the portal of her house ajar,
So that she may steal softly back unseen.
Now, were it slily clos'd behind her ——
      Senn. Well?
Bonav. There is but left, her ruin or to fly.
Luke! dearest Luke! I will be all my life
Bound to thee, wilt thou do me this slight office.
Senn. Hast thou then done? — Is this indeed thyself?
Speak'st thou of real purpose? Art thou truly
Pietro Bonaventuri? If thou art,
Then am I Luke Sennuccio; and no man
Durst ever call on me before to do
A thing so base.
   Bonav. Have patience!
     Senn. Hear now me.
If thou do not abandon this vile plan,
I will report thee to the lady's sire —
Or no! I will not put in risk thy life;

I will expose thee to Bianca's self.

Bonav. [*haughtily.*] Who gave you right to hold this talk
to me?

Senn. Nature, and threaten'd innocence, which finds
In every true man a defender.

Bonav. Luke!
I thought thou wast my friend.

Senn. I am thy friend.
Thou never hadst a truer. I dare say
Thou never wilt have one so true again.
For I will not, to pander to thy passions,
Stain thy immortal soul. I will not suffer
What doubtless now to thy distemper'd blood
Seems venial craft, but one day will appear,
When the film leaves thine eyes, atrocious guilt.

Bonav. Thou didst allow me honor.

Senn. I do still.
Said I not too, alas for human honor?
Alas, that somewhere it has aye some flaw!
Passion, ambition, indigence, all serve
To lend it pretexts to excuse its fall.
Thou, in the hunger of thy famish'd love,
Dost clutch at bread that is not fairly thine.
Thou shalt not have it.

Bonav. Thou dost bear me hard.
Thou art no lover, and thy cold resolve
Cuts off the last resource of both our lives.
For Blanche will pine to death, nor I survive.

Senn. So all youth think. And very few think right.

The storm blows, and the lily stoops her head,
But lifts it soon, and with the calm revives.
But, be it otherwise: hast thou not heard
Thou shalt not evil do that good may come?
Be honest, do thy duty: the result
Is with the All-Powerful, not the feeble will
Of circumscrib'd and narrowsighted men.
Pietro! end this matter as it may,
Thou art not sinless, knowing from the first
Well who thou art, which knew this virgin not.
Thou hast repair'd that error, like the brave
And honest soul thou art. Wilt thou fail now?
I will not think it. Get thee to thy chamber.
Ask if thou lov'st Bianca or thyself.
And on the altar of a true affection
Burn up thy guilty wishes. Angels will
Inhale with joy the incense, God approve
That truest hero, him who conquers self.

Bonav. [*Throwing himself on Sennuccio's breast, and with*
emotion.

O Luke! had I thy spirit!
           Senn. [*caressingly.*] And my blood?
Virtue, believe, is not to know not sin,
But the soul's victory when tried by sin.
Be thou thus virtuous, I will say thy love
Honors Bianca, were she born a queen.

[*Exit Bonav.*

Luke, leaning with his bent hand on the table, gazes
on him seriously as he retires. And Scene closes.

SCENE IV.

In the Casa Capello.
A room hung with portraits.   On a table, two lighted candles.

CAPELLO.   GOVERNESS.

Gov. I meant, your Excellence, to speak of this.
Cap. Hast thou then notic'd this sad change?   Since when?
Gov. 'T is some weeks gone since first my lady droop'd.
   I thought it nothing serious, still believing
   A little time would make all well again. —
Cap. Complain'd my daughter?   Sought she for no aid?
Gov. Alas! your Excellence, 't is not the body:
   This is some sore distemper of the mind.
Cap. What mean'st thou?
                    Gov. I would pray to be forgiven
   If I offend; but my young lady ——
                    Cap. Speak!
Gov. I fear, has something heavy on her heart.
Cap. Mean'st thou, in fine, my daughter is in love?
Gov. May it please your Excellence, 't is nothing less.
Cap. Be but the object worthy of her love,
   I were well pleas'd that it were nothing more.
   Who is it then?
                    Gov. Your Excellence must know
   My lady would not make of me her friend.

Cap. Thou art her governess: if, as I am loath
  To even conjecture, there is wrong in this,
  Thou only art to blame. Thou hast my child,
  Daily and nightly, under thy sole care.
  What can transpire that thou shouldst not observe?

Gov. Heaven is my judge, that I in this have done
  My proper duty. Till the last two days,
  I hop'd that all was well. But yesterday,
  Nor less the one before, the livelong night, *
  My dear young lady never press'd her bed,
  Walking unquietly from time to time
  Her chamber through.

                    Cap. And where wast thou the while?

Gov. Twice went I to the door. She thank'd me kindly,
  But bade me leave, as wanting not my help.

Cap. How is 't to-night?

                    Gov. She has retired early ;
  And all is quiet in her chamber. Haply
  She will sleep well to-night, being so much worn.

Cap. 'T is likely, very likely. God so grant!
  I will not break this salutary rest.
  But on the morrow bid her be prepar'd
  For solemn question. — O my darling child!

        He ceases to notice the GOVERNESS.

  Let not my colder age efface the sense
  Of my once passionate youth. When thou wast born,
  I pray'd *that* error of the old might not
  One day be mine. Yet is the lesson hard
  For a fond parent's heart! The child is his,

But not her passions. At the age when most
She needs his guidance, when new-born desire
Makes the first object welcome, and the soul
Takes cognizance of only things extern,
Then may he least command; then, child no more,
And yet not woman, she escapes his hand,
Before her unfledg'd sense has power to fly.
Hast thou done so, Bianca? Is this *love*
Which fevers thy young blood, then this unrest,
This secret sorrow marks a sense of shame,
Or unrequited or forbidden passion. See!——
Turning to the pictures. In so doing, he observes
the GOVERNESS.
Thou needst not wait, good Aia. It is now
Past midnight. Listen at my daughter's door,
Ere thou retirest; but disturb her not. — [*Exit Gov.*
Regards again the pictures.
Next to my father Carlo the ambassador's
Hangs thy sweet image, my Bianca! 'T is
One of the best from old Vecelli's hand.
How his soft pencil and his dulcet grace
Have beautified and made the canvas live!
The blood is in those cheeks! those eyes are moist!
From those just-parted delicate lips I seem
To feel the warm breath, and my own in turn
Might almost wave those airy threads of gold
That shape thy ringlets! Magic power of color!
Yet Titian vow'd thou didst surpass his art,
As did the light its symbol on his board.⁴

Such do not sigh in vain. Thou sorrowest then
For a forbidden passion which is shame ;
And my old house —— Thou shalt not dim its pride!
Forget thou the Capello, and a veil
Shall hide thy forfeit station, like Falier's,
Who too forswore his birthright. 'T is a thought
To keep me waking. Let me drive it hence.

     He lifts one of the candles towards the picture.

One nearer look, my child, before I go.

       Scene closes.

SCENE V.

A street, with a canal crossing it above; where, by a bridge which spans the canal, are obscurely seen, in the faint morning-twilight, the prows of gondolas. Forward, on either side the street, facing each other, the Casa Capello and the Casa Salviati.

From the portal of the latter Enter

BIANCA *and* BONAVENTURI, *the latter having a small dark-lant.rn, which he masks.*

Bian. See! the gray dawn! Farewell! A last —
Wo's me, I cannot say again — Farewell!
Bonav. [*pressing her to his breast.*
Haply, 't is not forever. Heaven bless thee!
Thy word remember.
                    Bian. Never, never, never
To be another's, if not thine. Farewell!
Embracing. BIANCA *crosses over to the palace on the right.
But almost instantly, coming back in terror:*
Ruin! ruin! O God! the door is clos'd.

Bonav. Hast thou no key?

     Bian. None, none! And if I had,
I durst not use it for the noise.

       Bonav. Stay here.
I will essay. Perhaps the door will yield.

Bian. No, no! Try not. There is no help but flight.

Bonav. Whither?

     Bian. Hast thou no parents?

       Bonav. Ay, but poor.

Bian. No matter; I can work. They shall be mine.
Come Bonaventuri! Come, my husband! Come!

Bonav. Alas, Bianca! all my worldly means
Lies in this little purse. The rest was given,
How gladly! for that first blest scene with thee
Which costs thee now so dear.

     Bian. Be it small or great,
It must be. My few rings will eke it out.
Tarry not. Every moment here is fraught
With more than death. I cannot face again
My father. Come. Art thou a man? Must I
Entreat thee to do that, which not long since
Thou wouldst have thought salvation?

       Bonav. 'T is for thee.
Wilt thou meet poverty and honest shame——

Bian. Rather than what awaits me here? That, that,
Canst thou ask that? O linger not! Each minute
Is so much lost to flight that must be quick.
For they will follow us. It is thy death.

Bonav. Come then, Bianca; now mine, life or death!
To the first gondola. Once out of Venice,
The first priest, if thou wilt, shall make us one.
Bian. Yes. O my father!
     Bonav. Hush, Bianca! Come.

He takes up the lantern.
They move up the scene in the shadow of the houses.

The Drop falls.

ACT THE SECOND

Scene I.   A chamber in the Pitti Palace at Florence.

THE GRAND DUKE

seated, leaning on a table in a pensive attitude.   MALO-
CUORE *standing apart, a little before him.*

Mal. [*in a tone of deferential inquiry.*
      My lord the Duke is not so well to-day.
                  A pause.
With still more deference.]
      Will my lord pardon his poor servant's zeal,
      And give command the hunt shall not take place?
G. D. [*without looking up.*
      For my ill-humor why should hundreds lack
      Their custom'd pleasure?   Let the order stand.
                  Again a pause.
Mal. 'T was from the last hunt that my liege came back
      With that strange sorrow which still wounds our hearts.
                  A longer pause.
G. D. Thou art a courtier, Malocuor.   Men say
      Thou hast sharp eyes, seest quickly and seest far.
      Thou boastest of thy zeal in our behalf.
      Forget thy art.⁵   What whisper stirs the court
      Touching our strangeness?

Mal. Some ascribe the cause
To depravation of the humors, bile,
Infarction of the spleen, — such natural ills;
Some to the weight of heavy cares of state ;
Others — your Highness bids that I should speak —
To discontent with your Archducal spouse.

G. D. [*hasti*'*y.*

They do me wrong : I hold her — in esteem.

Mal. Which often is the antipodes of love.

G. D. And to which guess does Malocuore lean ?

Mal. The last, with some admixture of the first.

Your Highness' malady is of the heart.

G. D. Ha ! — Men say well: thou hast keen eyes.

Mal. Would then
The royal patient deign to state his case,
Perhaps the surgeon might propound a cure.

The G. D. rises and walks to and fro.

G. D. [*after a pause.* ·

Hear then. —— But can I trust thee ?

Mal. Shall I prove
That I am worthy ?   Shall I state, myself,
Your Highness' symptoms, with the when and where,
And how, of the attack ?

G. D. What know'st thou ?   Speak!

Mal. 'T was at the last hunt.   As the cavalcade
Swept through the suburbs, and the people flock'd
To door and window to behold their Prince,
In a small cottage with a vine-clad porch,
That stood secluded where the highway turns,

Lean'd from a narrow casement next the roof,
A fair young creature of some eighteen years,
So strangely beautiful, and with a mien
So far above the seeming of her place,
The Great Duke, starting, drew his bridle short,
To gaze ——

    G. D. Art thou the Devil?   •

                    Mal. I am but
Your Highness' humble subject — with sharp eyes.
G. D. No more! Thou hast thy monarch's secret. He? —
Mal. His subject's instant aid, so he will deign
Graciously to command it.

                 G. D. Instant? Then
Sawest thou not, with all thy sight, what I
Saw and will vouch. This is no peasant maid,
Simple and uninstructed; far less one
Of that most numerous class in every life,
Whose vanity throws out perpetual lures,
Tempting temptation. Else the glance that pierc'd
Had made me whole. But thou dost not believe
In virtuous women?

              Mal. Ay, as in wall'd towns.
Many are strong, but none impregnable.
A vigorous siege and obstinate resolve
Will batter down or bring a Troy to terms.
Where open combat fails, some wooden horse
Lets in the troop that makes the stronghold ours.
Is it your Highness' will, this very day
The chance is given you to assault the place.

G. D. What sayst thou?

          Mal. Be it not ascrib'd a fault,

That I have dar'd anticipate your will.

G. D. Who gave thee orders?

          Mal. Will my lord but hear?

I have ventur'd only to make clear the approach,

By which your Highness might lay siege in form.

G. D. Speak plainly, Malocuor, and leave thy cant.

I like it not. Here is no vile intrigue;

And shall be none.

          Mal. Returning from the chase,

The Sovereign lifted up his eyes again,

Unto the cottage-window. But no more

The star was burning there that made the day;

And over his visage came like darkness. This,

When I saw this, and mark'd from day to day

The sadness lessen not; when, furthermore ——

G. D. [*impatiently.*

Well, well! we have admitted thou hast eyes.

Mal. Pardon, your Grace! — My spouse, by my command,

Made easily acquaintance with the dame

Who is this angel's mother, then herself.

She has seen her often, finds still some pretence

To do her kindness, — though, unlike the dame,

The daughter is both proud and strangely shy.

G. D. How speaks your spouse her bearing otherwise?

Mal. Modest, reserv'd; but, like her voice and mien,

Above her sphere.

G. D. And beauty?

    Mal. Marvelous.

G. D. [*taking his hand.*

 Ah, Malocuore! And this priceless maid? ——

Mal. So rarely worthy of a monarch's love;

 Has then my lord no wish to see her near?

G. D. Wouldst drive me mad? Speak on!

      Mal. No wish to be

 Beside her — and alone — and even now?

G. D. What! what! Thou didst indeed promise instant

  aid!

Mal. This very hour my spouse will bring her home.

G. D. To thine own house?

    Mal. To mine: my sovereign's house,

 Will he so grace it.   ·

    G. D. And this very hour?

   He rests his hand on MALOCUOR'*s shoulder.*

 Dear Malocuore! This is too much joy!

 What shall I do to compensate thy love?

 Thou hast indeed thy keen eyes us'd right well. —

 Thou wilt attend me. — Saidst thou not, this hour? —

 Bid come our Chamberlain. — [*Exit Mal.*

      How bright the day!

   Sitting down by the table.

 It seems to me as now I first had life.

   Rising, he passes through a door above, and

   Scene closes.

Scene II.

*In Malocuore's house.   The dressing-room of Signora Malo-
cuore.*

BIANCA.   *The* SIGNORA.

The latter displaying her jewels and finery.

Sign. You are a strange fair creature.   One would think
   These toys had been your playthings all your life.
   Yet that is not a long one either.
                  Bian. Why
   Should usage only breed indifference?   Rather
   It is the innate relish or distaste
   For such things makes them valued or despis'd.
   Age pranks itself therein like lighter youth.
Sign. You are a young philosopher.
                Bian. I know
   The difference betwixt folly and good sense.
   It were not wise in me to covet what,
   Even were 't attainable, would not fit my place.
Sign. That place may better; and these jewels then ——
Bian. Would still have little value in my eyes.
   I dress to please my husband; and his taste
   Is well contented with this simple garb.

Sign. In sooth, it does not misbecome you.   I have known
[*significantly.*
A sovereign prince to admire as plain a robe.
Pray let me hang this chain about your neck.
Thus, you are lovely.   Do not take it off.
It well relieves the ivory of that skin.

Bian. [*tranquilly removing the chain.*
But is in painful contrast to the rest.
Signora, to oblige my husband's mother
More than yourself, I have let you bring me hither.
Thanking your courtesy, suffer me to leave.

Sign. [*looking off the scene, as if hearing something.*
A little longer.   I have yet to show you,
Gentle Bianca, what is worth this all.
[*Exit.*

Bian. It must be greatly so, if thou wouldst dazzle
The rich Capello's child.   Capello!   Father!
Mourn'st thou Bianca yet?   Or has just anger
Stifled all sorrow for thy truant girl?
Who has one only grief, the thought that thou
Art unforgiving and yet unconsol'd.[6]

Enter

the GRAND DUKE — *eagerly,*
but becomes at once embarrassed, while BIANCA *looks*
surprised, but steady.

G. D. Pardon!   I —— [*stammering.*
Bian. Signora Malocuore

Has stepp'd out for a moment.

     G. D. The Signora

Shall be excus'd. Her absence gives me room

To make, without the encumbrance of a third,

The acquaintance of the loveliest of her sex.

Bian. This cannot be the master of the house.

G. D. The master's master, and your beauty's slave.

Bian. Ah! —   It is —— 'T is! I see now. The Grand

   Duke?

G. D. Francis of Medici, who —— Do not stoop!

  'T is I should rather kneel, wouldst thou permit,

  Fairest Bianca.

     Bian. Speak not so, my lord!

That tone becomes not either you or me. —

I have an earnest prayer to make your Grace.

'T is a small matter, but concerns me much.

G. D. Rise first. Now, what is there that thou canst ask,

  Saving his honor and his people's weal,

  That Francis will not grant? Think it then granted,

  So thou wilt one accord to me in turn,

  Bianca, and my love ——

     Bian. My lord! my lord!

I am — a marry'd woman.

     G. D. Marry'd? Well!

Am I not marry'd too? Alas! the heart

Cannot be bound so easily as the hand.

Bian. But the will may, and should when reason bids.

G. D. Reason now bids me to obey my will.

  The flame thy beauty kindled thy sense fans.

I had not heard thy speech, when on my eyes,
Lovely Bianca, ——

    Bian. Pardon me, my liege.
That I dare interrupt, impute it solely
Unto my duty, to you and to myself.
If I could ever listen, plac'd as now,
To such wild words as these from such as you, —
As I do not believe I ever should, —
Yet is my will not free as yours; my heart
Is, like my hand, my husband's.

      G. D. Every word
But adds new motive to my passion, showing
How rightfully 't is plac'd. Thou shouldst be silent,
Wouldst thou not foster feelings, which, in sooth,
Needed no nourishment.

    Bian. Then let me hence.
Such protestations — pardon me, my liege —
Demean yourself, your august spouse, and me.

     [*Offering to go. He stops her.*
G. D. Art thou insensible ? Thou art not vain.
But hast thou no compassion ?

      Bian. I have more.
You are my Prince, albeit I was not born
Your subject. Men report, and I believe,
You are among the noblest of crown'd heads.
My eyes have noted in your form and mien
What women value; and my ears have found
Sense in the tone and purport of your speech.
Thus amiable, thus gifted, so high-plac'd,

You cannot lack for dames in all your court
Fairer than your poor handmaid, noble too,
Who would joy in your homage, and respond
Haply unto your love, if — let me dare
To speak thus — you will do yourself that wrong
To offer it.

G. D. And are they such as thou?
Thy very words prove otherwise. If such,
They would not listen more than thou. No, thou,
Thou only, who, believe me! since these eyes
First saw thy fatal beauty, hast alone
Been mistress of my senses and my thoughts,
Thou only, fair ——

Bian. My lord, I must, I can not,
Will not listen longer. All the honor,
The reverence that I owe you, that I render;
But my first duty is to God. Permit me
Thus to perform it. [her hand on the door.

G. D. [stopping her.
No. If it must be,
'T is I will go. Bianca, have me not,
I pray, in disesteem. Let Francis hold
The next place in thy bosom, if thou canst,
To thy most happy husband. Thou shalt not
Say I abus'd my privilege. In love
I am like other men, and, loving so,
Like any gallant man I take my leave.

[Exit, bowing with sad deference.
Bian. A noble prince. Not conscious, surely, he

Of this vile plot. Ah! the arch-plotter comes.

Enter the SIGNORA, *with a casket.*

Sign. I have kept you too long waiting. Pardon. — Here
Is what will wake your wonder. [*opening the casket.*
            Bian. That was done
During your absence bravely. Shut the box.
Sign. What! Have you seen the Duke? I thought as
    much.
He often takes us by surprise. I hope
You have seiz'd the occasion, to present your prayer?
Bian. Was it for *that,* you urg'd me to come hither?
Sign. No. But I promised access to His Highness:
And I am happy, have you us'd this chance.
Sweet, look not grave: and do not haste away.
Bian. I do not like surprises: and this one
Has brought me no advantage. I will not
Trouble you longer.
        Sign. Nay, you shall not go
As you were angry. I shall see you home.
                [*Exeunt.*

SCENE III.

An Antechamber in the house of Malocuore.

Enter
from one side the G. DUKE, *as passing through,*
escorted by MALOCUOR.
The G. D. *stops short, laying his hand on his follower's arm.*

G. D. I have seen her, heard her, touch'd her.   All my
nerves
Tingle with pleasure.   Yet my heart is sad.
Mal. Is it that all is won?   Accomplish'd hope
Often brings sadness.
                 G. D. Since it nothing leaves
To feed expectance ? or, the goal once reach'd,
We find the prize not worth the strain and sweat ?
My longing is unsated, *my* bright prize
Grows brighter on my vision, like the sun
As day advances.   Yet my heart is sad :
For — all is lost.
            Mal. Then is it the first time
Your Highness has been vanquish'd.
                        G. D. The first time
Defeat is dearer to my heart than victory.
Thou look'st surpris'd.   I tell thee, Malocuor,

All thou hast said, all that thy spouse has told,
All that in heat of fancy I have dream'd,
Fall short to picture beauty, sense and worth,
That have no rivals save themselves. She is
The loveliest, best, and wisest of her sex.

Mal. May I infer, the most obdurate too?

G. D. What else? I said, "the best": and she is wed.

Mal. 'T is the first trial. When we shake the tree,
The apples fall not. But we lend our strength
To newer efforts; and they drop in time.

G. D. That is your over-ripe, and worm-gnaw'd fruit.
Bianca's stem is tough.

　　　　　　　Mal. Let royal favor.
Pour sunshine on the treasure of the tree,
The crude pulp mellows, and the stubborn stem,
Now useless, withers up. Invite the lady
To grace your Highness' Court.

　　　　　　　　　　G. D. That would I gladly.
But not to rot the virtue I admire.
The tree shall bear its honors in our midst,
And its fruit give out fragrance undespoil'd.
'T is something still to see her, hear her, know
That she is near me. Once beyond my reach,
I should be wretched, fearing she were lost.
Know'st thou her husband? To be lord of her,
He should be not ignoble.

　　　　　　　　　Mal. Not in mien.
The man is fair to look on, and well-spoken.
My lord might give him place about his person.

G. D. See it be done. Promise him what thou wilt,
  So it be not a place of public trust.
Mal. Your Grace shall be obey'd, and, more — be happy.
  They resume their way through the antechamber,
    MALOCUORE *ceremoniously conducting, and Exeunt.*

Scene IV.

*A poorly furnished chamber in the house of Bonaventuri's
Parents.*

BONAVENTURI. *His* MOTHER.

Moth. 'T is as thou sayest, Pietro, and our luck
  Is surely blossoming. And glad am I,
  If only for Bianca's sake, 't is so.
  To see that delicate creature, night and day,
  Toiling with those soft hands, that ne'er were made
  For menial labor, makes my heart bleed.
                          Bonav. Yet
  She does not murmur.
                    Moth. More an angel she.
  An angel is she. Oft I wonder, son,
  Though thou art brave and comely, thou couldst win

So rare a maiden.   But I wonder not,
Once won, thou gav'st up all to make her thine.
Bonav. She gave up all too, mother; and that all
  Was more a thousand times.
                                Moth. The heavier then
Her loss.   I fear she feels it so.   Her brow,
Methinks, grows sadden'd, and her cheek more pale.
I would she had less care on her young heart.
Bonav. What can we do?   Our money is all spent.
Until the Duke's protection be procur'd,
I dare not stir abroad to seek for work.
I wonder that Bianca was so bold
To gaze from window when the Court rode by.
Moth. 'T was but an instant, from the upper floor.
Thou shouldst not blame her.
                                Bonav. And I did not.   Yet
The risk was great.   And therefore I rejoice
In this court-lady's favor.   If nought else,
The Duke may shield us.   That is one care less.
Was not that wheels? [*listening.*
                                Moth. [*opening the casement.*
                The gracious dame herself,
In her brave equipage, has brought her back!
Bonav. She comes.   Bianca!

Enter BIANCA.
She throws herself into her husband's arms.

                                Bian. O, let us begone!

Bonav. Whither?   What is the matter?   Has the Duke
Refus'd his safeguard?

      Moth. Have you seen His Grace?

Bian. Yes, I have seen him, and will not again.
O Bonaventuri!   O my husband!

        Bonav. Speak! ·

What is it?

     Bian. Ruin!   Ruin, if we stay;
Hope, safety, happiness, all things in flight.
Let it be instant!

      Bonav. Whither?   And the means?

Venice can reach us elsewhere.   As well here.

Bian. No! not as well.   This place is bann'd of Heaven.
The world elsewhere is all for us to choose.

    BONAVENTURI *folds his arms about her as*
she hangs on his breast, — the MOTHER *looking on in*
speechless wonder, and

      the Drop falls.

ACT THE THIRD

· *Scene I. As in Act II. Sc. II.*

SIGNORA MALOCUORE.

Enter,
in festival dress, MALOCUORE.
He flings himself weariedly on a couch, without removing
his hat.

Mal. 'T is monstrous! Florence stands agape. Fools ask:
  Is this a Prince? or some great hostile king's
  High servant sent to ratify a peace?
  And wise men answer low: "Bianca's brother."
  Just as thou seest me, wearied unto death,
  So see a hundred nobles, dragg'd in state
  To swell the triumph of Vittorio, son
  Of a Venetian Senator. [*flinging his hat off in disdain.*
    Sign. And who
  But thou to blame? Of all thy fine-wove schemes
  To advance thyself, and stretch thy purse and mine,
  What is the upshot? O'er thee, step by step,
  Strides Bonaventuri; and the prude, his wife,
  Rides over me and all.
    Mal. Peace! Fret me not.

I am not now in mood.

        Sign. To list the truth?

'T is wholesome though. Thy aching bones are part

Of thy just penance; and my knotty facts

Shall lash thee to new virtue.

                 Mal. Well; proceed.

Only hear me in turn.

             Sign. Bianca houses

Not in the suburbs in a cottage now,

But near the *Trinità*, in palace-walls

That shame our own: her low-born husband rolls

In wealth beyond his trading master's, holds

His head above the nobles, with a pride ——

Mal. Will one day hurl him headlong. But his spouse

    Is gentle still. Why shouldst thou carp at her?

Sign. She treats me with an insolent disdain,

    Or looks me over.

             Mal. Ay; she knows thee well.

Sign. Ha!

    Mal. Was 't not thou that pander'd to the Duke?

Sign. At whose base prompting? If my palm is black,

    Thou art in to the elbow. Was it I

    That brought her to the Court? I had left her poor.

    Her natural pride' now swollen by all this pomp,

    With courtiers cringing at her dainty feet

    Who scarcely kiss'd the crown'd Joanna's hand,

    She trifles with the Duke, and plays the chaste,

    While he, the more she frowns, the more adores.

    Is not that so?

Mal. It is; but shall not be;
Though I deem not, as thou, Bianca feigns.
Sign. What new plan toward? [*disdainfully.*

    Mal. Thou knowest the hopes I built
On the bold Favorite's amour with the Princess?
Sign. The base was quicksand. So the fabric fell.
The dissolute Duchess makes the wife's cheek pale,
But not her heart. It still beats for her lord,
Or seems to.

    Mal. I have what will change its pulse. [*Going.*
If she resist this! —— [*holding up for a moment, at a
        distance, a sealed letter.*
    —— Even then I hope.
A mine will spring the tower which stands a siege.
          [*Exit.*
Sign. Subtle maligner! Thou mayst fathom man,
But hast no plummet to explore our sex.
Thou think'st I know thee not. Thou had'st better
  trust me!
Thy dallying with the Cardinal I see.
Beware! A crafty priest has double craft.
The mine thou digg'st against Bianca's faith
May split the rock whereon the miner stands.
       [*She turns, as going. And*

   Scene closes.

Scene II.

A room in the Old Medici Palace (the residence of Don Pietro.)

Isabella. Eleonora.

Isa. Content thee. That I fling away my hours
On Francis' pet, is not the man is bold,
Or young, or handsome — though I weigh the worth
Of all these qualities — but that I hate
His wife.
    Eleo. [*in great surprise.*
        I thought thou favoredst the Capello!
Isa. As thy dear lord, my brother does. In heart
I loathe her.
    Eleo. And for what?
            Isa. Because I loathe her.
What matters it? Not always do we know
Our cause of hate.
    Eleo. Not always care to know.
Isa. Or care to know. Be it as thou wilt. So say,
I am her rival; say, that men desert
Calypso's isle of dainties for the web
Of chaste Penelope; is 't not too much
The hypocrite should make both thee and me

Odious before our lords, and in the court
Teach men to estimate our freer lives
By her stiff model? Harmless as a dove
Fools may esteem her; but the serpent's wisdom
Prompts her mock coyness. If Joanna, whom
My brother Ferdinand so loves (because
Her weak spine promises the Duke no heir
That long shall live,) in her now-coming throes,
Which threaten peril, die, behold a chance
Bianca may improve!

        Eleo. Thou art not serious?

Isa. Our sire was, who in his later day
Married Camilla. She was not the peer
In beauty, worth, or birth of this Capello.
Francis has cloister'd her,[8] but not the less
Will do as his sire, mad for love as he.

Eleo. Ah! this is why the Cardinal and my lord
Precipitate the ripening of our plot.

Isa. It will not do. Bernard' Girolami,
The two Capponi, linger yet in France;
The Alamanni, Machiavelli, all,
Though eager, wait their secret coming, ripe,
Yet unresolv'd. The Cardinal —— But hush!
Here comes a doubtful friend. Eleonor',
Watch well your lips.

Enter MALOCUORE.

        What passes in the town,

Good Signor Malocuor?

          Mal. May it please your Grace,
The storm breaks not as yet ; but thunder rolls
At the horizon. Now the peace is over
Between the Cardinal and our Sovereign Lord,
His Eminence' agents stir the popular mind
With satires on the adventuress, and psalms
In praise of good Joanna, whose near death
Must come of Victor's triumph!⁹ The Capello
Will not go down to future times a saint,
If my lord's foes can help it. — Going hence,
Left my lord Cardinal any charge for me?
Isa. None. But be watchful. Thou wilt hear from him
Perhaps from Rome.

          Mal. I humbly take my leave.

             [*Exit — by the*
*side he had entered. The two princesses Exeunt by opposite side.*¹⁰

.

Scene III.

Room in the Pitti Palace.   As in Act II. Sc. I.

Grand Duke.   Don Pietro de' Medici.   Duke of
Bracciano.

The Grand Duke seated.

Brac. Your Highness has a twofold stake in this.
Your sister is my spouse, your insolent favorite —
So let me call him — is her open lover.
Does Isabella's conduct shame your House,
His prodigal pomp and measureless assumption
Wound your chief nobles' pride, and tempt your people
To mutiny, clamorous that they are not heard.
Don P. My liege and brother: Bracciano's words
Express his wish and motive: my resolve
Is fix'd.   Eleonora shall not make
My name a byword.
       G. D. [*rising.*] That thyself hast done.
Thy wantonness and license are unmatch'd.
Nor canst thou fling one stone against thy spouse
Should not rebound on thee.
              Don P. My luxury
Is not fed from thy treasure.   For my spouse,

The Archduchess' wrongs are not so secret.

     G. D. Ha! —

Brother, the cleft betwixt us yawns too wide

To need distension. This much is to say:

I would not have the Duke of Alba wroth.

Eleonora's death ——

    Don P. May drive him mad.

What then? it is my quarrel, none of thine.

I reck not the Toledos. Mov'd I not

Don Pedro in this matter? With what boot?

He let not even his sire, Garzía, know,

But screen'd his strumpet sister in my spite.[11]

 *

The G. Duke *walks up and down a few moments*

 in anxious thought, then, turning to the

   Duke of Bracciano:

G. D. Orsini, will it not suffice for thee

 To shut up Isabella? Cloister'd life

 Leaves her repentance, yet concludes thy shame.

Brac. But gluts not vengeance. Sure, my liege o'erlooks

 The Orsini's honor.

    G. D. Not so, Duke, not so.

Have not the Medici shed blood enough

Of kindred veins? Wouldst thou exact this too?

She was my father's darling. It is hard.

 Walks up and down with signs of agitation.

  Then, addressing both:

For Bonaventuri — Let me frankly speak :
I trust to both your honors — If I wink
At his egregious folly, think ye then
My pleasure goes with my forgiveness? No,
He should have died ere this; but men would say —
I slew him to ascend Bianca's bed.

Don P. We will provide for that, so thou wilt promise
To hold us not to answer for the deed.

The G. D. stands thoughtful for a moment.

G. D. Pietro, our brother Don Giovanni died
Like righteous Abel. The assassin fell,
Stabb'd by his father, in his mother's arms.
I will not imitate my brother's crime,
Nor my stern father's vengeance.
                              Brac. And for me?
G. D. My sister is thy spouse. I cannot punish
What, plac'd as thou, I might myself have done.
                    [*He bows in sign of dismissal, and*
                              Exeunt Don P. and Brac.

The GRAND DUKE *looks after them a
moment thoughtfully, then moves slowly towards the
chair — and scene changes to*

SCENE IV.

A magnificent room in the palace of Bonaventuri.

Enter BONAVENTURI,
leading in with great animation SENNUCCIO,
who follows with marked reluctance.

Bonav. Welcome once more! A thousand, thousand times,
Welcome to Florence! Make this house thy home.
Command me every way. Why art so grave?
Thou wouldst have fled me in the public street.
Couldst thou then think Pietro could be else
To Luca than Pietro?
    Senn. Yea. And there
Perhaps I did thee wrong. But elsewhere too?
Why didst thou flee from Venice? That bad scheme
Thou wouldst persuade me to? ——
    Bonav. [*changing color.*] Dost ask me *here*,
If I be lawful master of my own?
Senn. No; for thou art not. Thou didst steal thy wife.
Bonav. Sennuccio, I bear much from thee.
      Senn. Is 't not
True thou didst rob the old man of his child,
When thou didst suffer me to think thou wouldst not?
Bonav. But not to beggary I bore her. Lo!

The amends is ample, and the sire appeas'd.
This day thou sawest her brother, like a prince
Attended, ride in triumph to my house;
Where he now gladly dwells.

Senn. The more his shame,
Knowing how it was got.

Bonav. Thou dar'st! ——

Senn. Not say
One word that is not truth.   Wilt thou maintain
This palace was given by the Duke to *thee?*

Bonav. I do.   It is my meed, and fits my place.
I have risen in his service step by step.
All know I am his Favorite.

Senn. And thy wife?

Bonav. His Grace adores her.   But that hurts her not.

Senn. No?   Yet they say in Florence ——

Bonav. What is said?

Senn. [*hesitating, then, slowly.*
She is to Francis, what Camilla was
To Cosmo ere he wed her.

Bonav. 'T is a lie!
The atrocious slander of the Grand Duke's foes,
Led by the intriguing Cardinal.   Bianca
From the first warn'd me — still would have me fly.

Senn. Yet thou remainest? —[*looking at him with aston-
ishment.*
Let me see thy wife.

Bonav. Gladly.   Come now.   Thou then wilt do me right.
Thou then ——

Enter a PAGE.

Well?

Page. Be not angry, sir! The note
I was bearing to the Duchess, by mischance,
Or stolen, is lost. I am sure 't is not my fault.
I miss'd it only when I reach'd the door.

Bonav. Thou art very careless. Get thee back at once.
Tell to her Highness thy mishap, and say,
I will be shortly with her Grace. [*Exit Page.*
— Now, Luke.
[*about to lead him off.*

Senn. Stay yet. What is this Duchess? I have heard
Strange tales to thy dishonor. Men assert,
The dissolute Isabella ——
Bonav. [*with confusion, yet with vanity.*
O a freak!
Her Highness shows me favor.
Senn. As she does
Her lord's own kinsman. Have a care! Thou goest
Straight to thy fall. Beware the Orsini!
Bonav. [*impatiently.*] Come.

As he is leading SENNUCCIO *off,* BONAVENTURI *stops.*

Say nothing of this letter to Bianca.
Senn. She then? ——
Bonav. Still loves me dearly. It might grieve her.
Senn. And is that true? Then thou deserv'st to fall.
[*Exeunt.*

SCENE V.

Another Apartment in the Same.

BIANCA *discovered in a dejected attitude.*

Bian. And this is splendor! this is pleasure! this
The world calls happiness! Would I could exchange
All that is now for what alone was ours,
When in that humble home I toil'd all day,
As never yet my father's handmaids toil'd!
Then slept I well; my cheek was pale indeed,
But not with sorrow; for my husband's heart
Was all my own. [*Comes forward.*
     And is it no more mine?
Haply, his vanity alone is mov'd.
Wealth, luxury, the notice of the great,
All swell his pride. Alas! he will not see
There be distinctions which are far from honor.
Sure of my heart, which well he knows is his,
He glories in the Duke's mad passion, and counts
Its harvest only, reckless that the world
Deems it is gather'd from his partner's shame.
He comes. And with a stranger.
    Enter BONAVENTURI *and* SENNUCCIO.
        A grave face

That pleases me.

Bonav. Bianca, welcome bid

To Luke Sennuccio, my old Venice friend.

Bian. All of my husband's friends are welcome here.

But a true friend, as I have heard you call'd,

Sits next my heart. From heart then welcome, sir.

[giving her hand.

Bonav. Adieu, awhile. Bianca, I have wrung

Consent from Luke to make his quarters here.

Senn. But ——

Bonav. Nay, revoke not! I shall hold thee bound.

Keep him engag'd, love, till my soon return. *[going.*

Bian. Why must thou go? Must it be every night?

Bonav. 'T is nothing— a mishap. 'T is not for long.

[Exit hastily.

SENNUCCIO *looks after him with indignation,*

and with pity on BIANCA.

Bian. [*observing the look.*

Pray, mind me not. I ought not to be vex'd.

I —— [*Recovering with an effort.*

Sir, you are fresh from Venice. Left you then

The Adriatic in my brother's train?

Senn. No, I have idled in my native town

Some days.

Bian. And came not once to see my lord?

O Signor! And he thought so much of you!

Senn. I knew not that his feelings were not chang'd.

The gay, rich courtier, favorite of the Duke,

Was not my fellow-clerk of former days.

Bian. You do him wrong; his heart is still the same.
Have you not found it so?

    Senn. But could I know it?
What gave me right to press on his new fortune
The reminiscence of a rusty time?

Bian. Old friendship, and the knowlege you had had
Of his brave heart.

    Senn. Alas, Signora! when
I saw in mien the outward man so chang'd,
Needs must I credit what the people said.

Bian. What said they? Tell me!

    Senn. Can you bear the truth?

Bian. Your quality of plainness I have heard of;
Oft, for my husband's sake, have wish'd it near.
I hear nought but from lying lips; my eyes,
They serve me, painfully and well. What say
The folk of Bonaventuri?

    Senn. Let me first,
Signora, put a question. Is it true,
That you have pray'd your husband flee from here?

Bian. It is, I think, my daily prayer.

    Senn. And why?

  A pause.

Bian. Here is not safe for either him or me.

Senn. [*solemnly.*] It is not safe for either you or him.

Bian. What mean you? Ah! 't is this that I would ask.
What say the people of us; of us both?
The wrong they do my honor can I help?
It is his will, and I submit to bask me

In the hot sunshine of the Court. But oh!
For the old shadow of my humble life!
Not for my father's roof — I would not be
Other than wed, — but for the humble shadow
Where liv'd my husband all in all to me,
For I to him was all! [*weeps.*

    Senn. And is it now
Too late for this?

    Bian. For him — not me. He loves
Too well the pomp of this most wretched life.
Senn. Wretched indeed! where every breath he draws
Is deadly-perilous to himself, and blasts —
Pardon! — the good name of his spouse.

    Bian. 'T is frank.
This thou hast heard. This is the common fame
I too have learn'd to read in all I see;
For not a whisper yet invades my ears.
I read it in the wicked eyes, that flash
Malignant triumph when not bent on mine,
Then suddenly, when my gaze encounters theirs,
Look meek as angels', or grow loving-soft.
I know how busy are the Grand Duke's foes.
They sow thick calumnies, and the poison-seed
Will sprout when I am dead. Bianca's name
Shall be enroll'd with all that in her sex
Is impudent, artful, — it may be, debauch'd;
And all because the husband that she lov'd
Was weak.

   Senn. And selfish.

Bian. No, no; say not that!
His heart is good: he knows not that I suffer.

Enter a PAGE.

Page. The Signor Malocuore.
            Bian. Let him wait. [*Page about to go.*
Senn. Rather, I take my leave. [*going.*
            Bian. Go not, I pray.   •
Believe me, I have not known such relief,
Not since this weary prison-life at Court.
Or, if you will go, you will soon be back?
You will not disappoint my husband's hope
And mine?
         Senn. I will not: for you are sincere.
Lady, for your sake, here a day or two
I will sojourn.
         Bian. So you shall make these walls
To me more sufferable. [*Exit Sennuccio, bowing with
        an air of deep respect and sympathy.*
To Page.] Show the courtier in. [*Exit Page.*
A brave good man! How his unburnish'd gold
Makes vile the tinsel of such knaves as this!

Enter MALOCUORE.

Mal. Most excellent lady! if I should intrude ——
Bian. At this unwonted hour for him, what brings
The Grand Duke's confidant?

Mal. The present matter
Looks rather to your honor'd spouse, than you.

Taking from his vest a letter.

This writing is his hand, I think. The address
Is known to you. [*gives it.*

BIANCA *regards the letter with agitation ;*
MALOCCORE *watching her with ma'ignant pleasure.*

Bian. [*with an effort.*] How came this to your hands ?
Mal. What matters it ? The purport you will find
Concerns you nearly.

    Bian. [*recovering, and with sternness.*
      Brought it you for that ?
And hop'd you I would read it ? [*flings the letter on a*
              table.

      Mal. Hop'd you would,
In justice to yourself, here ascertain
The measure of your wrongs.

    Bian. [*with increasing severity and with scorn.*
      That with your master
I might consent to right them !

      Mal. The redress
Lies with yourself, Madonna. But, to know
How grossly you are cozen'd by your lord ——

Bian. Sir, touch him not ! It is a dastard's part
To vilify the absent.*

    Mal. [*discomposed. Then, gravely :*
     I have done

My duty toward a lady whom I honor,
My lord adores, and my own spouse holds dear.

                                [about to go.

Bian. And has your duty further prompted you
To ope this missive? [*lifting it.*

                Mal. [*commanding himself.*

             See, madam, for yourself.
The silken thread, the seal, are still unbroken.

Bian. Then shall they so remain. [*She holds the letter in the*
                              flame of a candle.

        Mal. What would you do?

Bian. Destroy forever what 't would shame my lord
To think I knew of, and prevent in you
The hope that in your absence I would read it.
'T is done.   You know me better now.   Good night.

               [*Exit — with an expression of*
                   deep despite — Mal.

Oh Bonaventuri!   And for thee, for this,
I gave up all! [*clasping her hands in anguish.*

        My heart! my heart! my heart!

           [*Buries her face in her hands,*
                   sobbing. And

Scene closes.

SCENE VI.

A street, having others crossing it.
It is starlight.   On the right, a whiter portion of the sky
shows the moon to be rising.

Enter
SCHERRO, MASNADIERE, SCHERANO, MALANDRINO,
and other ASSASSINS.

Sgher. Scherano, Malandrino, get you quickly
    To the Orsini palace, for the task
    That 's laid out there.   The knave that keeps to-night
    The gate will smooth your way.   Whisper my name. —
    Make a clean job.   You are to use no weapons.
    Ply but your fingers.
                    Malan. Captain, let me stay.
    Here is more manly work.
                    Sgher. But pays no better.
    Why, thou art nice !   Is not Bravone gone
    To Cafaggiolo, with the bold Lucchesan,
    To rid Don Pietro of his Spanish wife ?
Malan. But hast thou men enough ?   The fop, they say,
    Is full of mettle ; and the two stout fellows, .
    That follow him, look as they would use their swords.
Scher. One of them may.   The other is bought off.

Sgher. Which makes us six to two. They must indeed
Be devils to match us. To thy proper work.
[Exeunt Scher. and Malan.
Here comes a lantern. 'T is our game. This way.
The Assassins secrete themselves in one of the cross streets.

Enter
BONAVENTURI, *preceded by* BRENNA *with a lantern,*
and followed by CAGNOTTO: *both well-armed.*

Bren. We are beset! *[falling back on the others.*
Bonav. Stand by me, men.
Bren. [running off.] Not I!
They are two to one. *[Exit.*
Bonav. Base coward!
Cagnot. Traitor rather:
He has carried off the light.
Bonav. We shall not need it.
The moon is o'er the houses' tops enough
To let us see their blades. They are on us now.
Back to the wall, Cagnotto.

During this dialogue, the ASSASSINS,
who had spread themselves out so as to prevent escape,
come forward, SGHERRO *in advance, to the two,*
who stand with their backs to the wall.

Sgher. [to Cagnotto.] Get thee gone.
One is our man. That is not thou.

Cagnot. [*cutting him down.*] It is

For thee.

An Assassin. Thou hast made me Captain.   Thanks!

[*wounding Cagnot., who falls.*

Cagnot. Master, I have done you service.   See me paid.

[*Dies.*

Bonav. [*running the assassin through.*

'T is done, my brave.   So. [*disabling another.*

Halt, you other three !

What would you ?   Money ?   Take it.   Let me hence,

And ten times o'er the amount is yours to boot.

Masn. Coin thy blood into ducats if thou wilt,

'T is in thy veins alone we seek them.   Thus.

All three remaining Assassins rush on BONAVENTURI *at once,*

who, after an animated resistance and repeated

wounds, falls.

Bonav. Bianca!   Thou 'rt — aveng'd !

Masn. The Orsini too.

Quiet ? [*leaning over the body.*

Assass. This will make sure. [*raising his weapon.*

Masn. No!   'T is enough.

He has fought bravely, and our work is done.

The Moon, now risen over the houses' tops,

throws its light upon the group.

The Assassins disperse, leading off their wounded comrade, and

Scene closes.

SCENE VII.

In the Orsini Palace.   The bedchamber of Isabella.

ISABELLA *asleep.*
Beside the bed, on a stand, a taper and a silver hand-bell.

Enter, a-tiptoe,
SCHERANO *and* MALANDRINO.
They speak in an under-tone.

Scher. Shall I awake her ?
                    Malan. No, 't is better thus.
Going to the bed.] A most fair creature !
                              Scher. Let us wake her then,
And hear her prayers. What ho ! Your Highness ! Up !
Isa. Who are you ?   Ah ! [*she starts up and rings the bell.*
                    Scher. Cry, ring.   There are no ears.
The Duke has taken especial care of that.
Isa. [*wildly.*] Has my lord sent to murder me ?
                                   Malan. Even so.
Isa. Let me escape !   I am not fit to die.
I will make you richer far than he will do.
My brothers too will heap wealth on you both.
Scher. Which of them ?   Don Pietro's wife even now
By her lord's will is going where you shall go.

Isa. [*sinking back.*] Accursed House of Medici!

        Scher. Ay, so

Say I! Amen! I would we were well-rid

Of all the race.

    Isa. Have mercy! Take this ring.

'T is worth a thousand ducats.

      Malan. [*taking it.*] 'T will not save you.

Scher. Quick to your prayers. Your lover by this time

Is well carv'd up.

     Isa. Troilo Orsini?

      Malan. No,

Bonaventuri.

Isa. [*falling back again.*] God is just!

  Scher. [*pressing a pillow over her face.*] Why so;

'T is a good prayer. — Thou dost nought, Malandrino!

Malan. [*sullenly.*

My hands were made to clutch an iron sword-hilt,

Not to choke women.

    Scher. Only take their rings.

'T is nice distinction!

     Isa. Oh!

     Scher. What! not yet done?

Thou art strong, to be so fair. [*A pause. He lifts the*

               pillow.

      Still now.

     Malan. Come then.

I 'd rather kill ten men than do this over.

      Exeunt — Malan. looking back

    upon the bed, as he moves.

SCENE VIII.

In Bonaventuri's palace. As in Scene V.

BONAVENTURI *lying on a couch.*
At his head, one on either side, the Court Physicians
BALDINI *and* CAPPELLI. BIANCA *kneeling*
by the Couch, holding his
hand clasped in hers. SENNUCCIO *standing at*
the foot.

Bian. Thou shalt have justice ! Thou shalt hear it vow'd
By his own lips! Thy spirit shall go down,
Unto the biding-place of all the dead,
Appeas'd ! Vittorio will bring back the Duke.
He has pray'd me test his friendship. I have kneel'd
But once for favor ; I will kneel once more,
And thy poor bleeding wounds, belov'd Pietro,
Shall cry with me for vengeance. —
         Bonar. [*feebly.*] He will come —
Too late : my life — ebbs fast.
         Bian. Have mercy, God !
Sustain him yet awhile, renown'd Baldini !
Master Cappelli,[12] is all art in vain ?
Bald. [*feeling the wrist of the hand Bianca abandons to him.*
Alas, Signora ! all that art can do

Is now to watch its own prognostications
Fatally realiz'd.

        Capp. [*feeling the other wrist.*

           If your honor'd spouse,
Lady, has aught at heart he fain would utter,
Let him be quick. This draught will give him strength,
Yet a brief space. [*Bonav. drinks.*

        Bonav. Bianca! ——

              Bian. [*kissing his hand.*

              Speak, beloved!
Thy will shall be my law.

            Bonav. [*reviving.*

               Canst thou — forgive me?
Bian. Thou hast done no wrong; none that I ever ponder'd
With aught but sorrow — sorrow for thyself.
Bonav. Thou knowest not all. That night — we fled from
      Venice ——
Raise me. — Still higher, Doctor. Thank you. — Then,
When on the stairs I left you — to make sure,
I said, that all was safe — I stole away
To — shut the portal of your father's house,
That barr'd return for aye. Breath! breath, O God!

      BONAVENTURI, *panting. — A brief pause.*

Bian. Be sooth'd. 'T was passion made thee to forget
Duty and honor. I have not repented,
Save for my father's sake, to have fled from home.
I have liv'd happy, till — till ——

Bonav. Till I wrong'd thee.

I am justly punish'd. Seek not — to avenge me.

Sennuccio —— Oh! — The draught! the draught,
    Cappelli!

         Drinks again. *Pause.*

Quickly! My last sand 's running out. Bianca —

Take to thy heart — Sennuccio. A true friend,

He did abhor my — treachery. Let him be —

Warmly commended — to my lord the Duke.

He will — well serve him — as I — ne'er have done.

    Enter VITTORIO CAPELLO.

Bian. [*starting up eagerly.*

    Is his Grace coming?

         Vitt. News had reach'd the Palace,

The Lady Isabella and the spouse

Of Don Pietro suddenly were dead. —

Bonav. Murder'd! — Heaven's justice! — Murder'd!

    Falls back, gasping, into the arms of the attendants.

         Vitt. The Grand Duchess,

Hearing, was seiz'd with travail premature,

And cannot live beyond the hour.

    The Physicians, already in excitement,
hastily resigning BONAVENTURI *to* SENNUCCIO, *make for*
the door, but pause on the sill, as BONAVENTURI,
springing up half-erect, exclaims to BIANCA:

Bonav. My star
Is set! I see — ascend the whitening sky,
Lord of the day — thy planet! Hail, Grand Duchess!
                    Falls back.
Thus — Bonaventuri's murder — is aveng'd —
And thou — art recompens'd. [*Dies.*
                    Senn. It is all over.

With a piercing shriek, BIANCA
throws herself upon the body. The PHYSICIANS,
one instant more lingering, hurry from the scene.
VITTORIO, *with hands folded, looks from the foot of*
the couch upon the corpse, and SENNUCCIO
at the head bends over it, and
slowly

The Drop falls.[13]

ACT THE FOURTH

Scene I. A saloon in in the Pitti Palace.

DONNA VIRGINIA and SIGNORA MALOCUORE.

Sign. How does your Highness like her for a sister?
Virg. Well.
 Sign. Well? ' But for a mistress?
        Virg. Even as much.
 I find her nothing chang'd. Our Sovereign Lady
 Is the Signora Bonaventuri still.
Sign. Ay, so I think her. She can never be
 Aught but the widow of a banker's clerk.
Virg. But that is not my meaning. She was ever
 'More than the Favorite's wife. A noble lady,
 Who still has been the pattern of our sex, —
 Whose virtues have no rivals but her graces, —
 And those scarce match'd. My brother has done well.
 Did not the proud Republic this day crown her
 Their royal daughter, she were still his peer.
Sign. You do surprise me. Have her witch's-arts
 Enchanted too your Highness? [11]
       Virg. You forget,
 Signora Malocuor, of whom you speak.
 The Grand Duke's bride, Bianca, has no arts

Save those which nature taught her.   I had thought
.   The rabblement alone believ'd such tales.
Sign. I did but jest.   I was, knows not your Grace?
Donna Bianca's first and fastest friend.
Well pleas'd am I to find your Highness' heart,
So far as the young prince, Don Cæsar's right
Permits, is given so well.   But may I ask,
Does the Grand Duchess give hers in return?
Virg. She does to all who love her.   Even her foes
May boast her kindness.
                    Sign. Yet your Highness' mother —
Pray pardon me — is pining, cloister'd still.
Virg. That is my brother's fault, not hers.
                    Sign. She has
The power however to move that brother's heart.
She us'd it for the Cardinal, her foe.
Why not for you?
                    Virg. My mother was as kind,
And for the Cardinal did what she has done,
Open'd the royal coffers.   Why has not
The Cardinal, who pretends to love my mother,
In gratitude mov'd the Duchess to this act?
Sign. Haply for that he knew it were in vain.
Virg. I will essay.   In this high festal time,
Fill'd to the brim with joy and happy pride,
The Duke's heart may flow over ——
                    Sign. But not hers.
Virg. [*without noticing the interruption.*
— And the rich superflux make glad the heart

Of Cosmo's lonely widow. — Do not stir.

[*as Sign. attends her going.*

I need you not, Signora. [*Exit.*

Sign. [*returning, after seeing Virginia ceremoniously through
     the door.*]   Why not say :

" Of the Grand-duchess dowager " ?   Artless fool !

That hast a child's heart with a woman's head.

The daughter of Camilla, thou dost well

To take Bianca's part : thy upstart dam

Was such another mushroom, vain and proud,

And beautiful as she.   Come but the day

That Ferdinand shall mount his brother's throne,

The fate of the new Duchess is like hers, —

Or haply worse, for the proud Churchman hates her.

And yet — methinks — he loves her too, with love

After his fashion, like his father's son.

I must watch this.   Camilla freed or not,

St. Mark's new daughter shall not win thereby. [*Exit.*

SCENE II.[15]

A hall in the same.

Enter,
from opposite sides,
DON PIETRO *and the* ARCHBISHOP OF PISA.
The latter stopping ceremoniously for the Prince to pass,
DON PIETRO *goes up to him.*

Don P. Well met, Archbishop. 'T is a glorious day
For the Capello.
        Archb. And for you, my lord ?
Don P. Even as you see. I, with the bastard John,
Marshal'd the guard of honor at the Gate
Right willingly. By Heaven! it was a show!
You, who with Abbioso and the rest
Met at Firenzuöl the pompous train,[16]
Can witness that. And when the pageant pass'd
Between our glittering lines, amid the roar
Of cannon, and the peal of all the bells,
I thought how Cardinal Ferdinand would wince :
And that was joy for me.
        Archb. Alas, my lord!
That you will visit with this evil will
Your pious brother !

Don. P. My pious brother! Is 't
Of Cosmo's son you speak? Or think you well
I take for holy all a Churchman's cap,
Mitre or hat may cover? You do right
Perhaps to love him. 'T was his hand that laid
The first step in your scale of fortune. What
Have I to thank him for? That he was got
Before me? He has cause to dread, and hates,
Bianca: she may bear Francesco sons.
I have no cause for either fear or hate.
Dies the Grand Duke without heirs male, upstarts
My Cardinal brother, doffs the purple, and takes
His coveted place. Sometimes he makes me blind
To his dark views, and presses me to marry.
But now and then comes daylight, and I see
Clearly — as now.

     Archb. Your Grace will yet admit
His Eminence is sincere, when once consider'd
'T is not the Duke's new marriage is oppos'd,
But marriage with the Intendant's widow, unmeet
For Cosmo's heir and Cosmo's ancient blood,
Unmeet to follow union with the House
Of Hapsburg. To succeed the late Grand Duchess,
The Emperor Rodolph gladly had bestow'd
A child of Archduke Charles. Such match had pleas'd
My lord the Cardinal.

     Don P. Think you so? What then?
What is our blood that it should scorn Capello's?
Is it so many more than tenscore years,

Since Averado, son of the Lucchesan,
Portion'd his mighty fortune, got by trade,
Between his six sons? whence arose our House.
Not then the triple flower-de-luce emblaz'd
The middle roundle of our shield in chief.
Our power was all, — nor that without dispute;
Our rank a usurpation; and our title?
Why, know not all men, fifty years agone
Our beast still ramp'd where gleams the lilied crown?[17]
God's might! the throne of Clement's bastard son,
Founded by perfidy on public wrong,
Is all too new, that his unlineal heirs
Should in the second generation vaunt
A scarce-acknowledg'd royalty.[18]   'T is trick!
By holy John, as patent as this hand!
Did Ferdinand scorn Camilla? Yet was she
No equal of Bianca. Lo, this day,
Adopting her the daughter of the State,
The proud Republic crowns our Duchess queen,
Peer of the Queen of Hungary and her
Who sat in Cyprus. Why is he displeas'd?
Because her lord is Cosmo's eldest son.
Camilla could not bear a male should be
His senior. No, Archbishop, it is not
The Archduchess Ferdinand would choose, but one
He knows the Grand Duke would not choose.

Archb. My lord,
I cannot credit this. The Cardinal Prince
Is holy.

Don P. You may say so. But you are
A man, Del Pozzo, of no common mind.
You know the Cardinal is a worldly prince
And an unmatch'd dissembler.

Enter ABBIOSO.

Is 't not so,

Good Bishop?
    Abb. Pleases it your Grace to speak
Of what and whom?
      Don P. Of my pure brother, pious
Cardinal Ferdinand. Holdst thou him a saint?
Abb. My opinion of the Cardinal is known.
I love him not.
    Don P. With reason. Late at Rome
He holp to make St. Peter's Vicar loath
To hoist thee to the half Pistoian see:
Ah, Abbioso? Get thee quickly hence
To the Lagunes. In thy new function there,
Bland Secretary, serve thy liege lord Francis,
Near the Pregádi.¹⁹ Here thou shalt not quarrel
With Holy Church.
    Archb. I would, your Grace, that none
Might quarrel here. Our sovereign is the lord
Of his own will. What pleases him to do,
In his born right, that should content us also.
And with a virtuous and high-bred fair dame,
As is our Lady, even the Cardinal must

In time be pleas'd.

   Don P. So let him be or not.

Philip of Spain approves.   Though Austria murmur,

Spite the whole College and the Pope to boot

Others will show like sense. —   But time calls off.

We must prepare us to attend in pomp

The solemn crowning of the titular Queen,

And the renew'd high nuptials. How will like

Your Cardinal that?

    Abb. He has sent *one* gentleman

To watch the game and make report; himself

Too busy with affairs of Heaven to come.

Don P. An impotent insult. Laugh you not, Archbishop?

Archb. I know nought impotent in the hand or head

  Of the lord Cardinal. [*Exit Don Pietro.*

    Abb. No; nor in his fangs.

The Medici are venom'd serpents all.

Archb. Have care, Ottavio! I am known no traitor,

  Or thou hadst never risk'd that thrust.

     Abb. I hope

The new-create Grand Duchess may not prove

Its point prophetical. Let her, I say,

Beware the Cardinal Medici's venom'd fang![20]

      [*Exeunt at opposite sides.*

SCENE III.

The Grand Duchess's Apartment in the same.

BIANCA, *magnificently arrayed, but without the royal mantle.*
VIRGINIA, *who has her hand in Bianca's.   On their
right, a little behind, Bianca's daughter* PELLEGRINA *with
her husband* BENTIVOGLIO.   *On the left, at a like distance,* SIGNORA MALOCUORE.

Enter
CAPELLO, *with the* PATRIARCH *of* AQUILEIA.
Behind them, VITTORIO.

Bian. It shall be so, Virginia.   Doubt it not.
          VIRGINIA *retires beside the* SIGNORA — *on whom she
                    looks triumphantly.*
    O my dear father!   Uncle!   May I deem
    This day makes full requital for the past?
²¹ The sorrow that I caus'd thee, the dishonor
    Brought, though I meant it not, upon thy House?
Cap. No more of that, my child.   'T was not thy crime.
    The good Seunuccio has disclos'd me all.
    Know'st thou, Bianca — did thy brother tell thee,
    How I had hung thy picture all with black,
    That day I lost thee? how the veil was drawn,
    When the Duke's favor shining on thy spouse

Made him thy equal?   But when Sforza came,
Praying the Senate to receive as son
Of Venice the Great Duke himself; and when,
Like Catharine Cornaro, thou wast made
The Child of the Republic, and a Queen;
Then did I cause a crown surmount the frame.
But 't was not needed: Titian, had he liv'd,
Had pointed to the air of native pride [22]
That dignifies thy beauty, and had said:
" Superfluous decoration!   Nature gave
A better diadem.   And that I drew.
Lo, where in every trait the destin'd Queen! "
Is it not true, Grimani?   O my child!
Thou wast my darling ever, my best joy;
Thou art my glory now, my House's pride.
Patr. The will of Heaven works oft by humble ways.
That jewel his bold subject stole and wore
The Duke hath made the centre of his crown.
Keep thou, O gem, thy lustre without flaw!
So shall the people bless thee. — Francis comes.

Enter
the GRAND DUKE, *attended by* SENNUCCIO.
The G. D. is splendidly attired, but without his robes of
state.   SENNUCCIO also, like all the other
persons present, is in full costume as for some
extraordinary occasion of Court-festival.

G. D. Good morrow, friends.— Bianca! My fair Queen! —

SENNUCCIO, *with* CAPELLO, *&c., takes his*
place with the other personages in the background.
How well this pomp becomes thee!   Thou art now
A jewel fitly set.   And yet, believe,
Thy lustre shines not more in Francis' eyes
Now than that morn, when, from the little window,
Like a rich picture in a sorry frame,
That sweet face dawn'd a moment on his gaze;
Not more ador'd than when, a twelvemonth since,
Thy heart first open'd to the houseless love
That long had knock'd in vain to be let in.
Yet do I joy, for thy sake, joy for mine,
[23] Joy for the offspring, hope of which I nurse
For my throne's heritage, our love's glad contract
This day shall ratify before the world,
And thou, whose worth needs not the gilt of rank,
Shalt by thy country, even for that worth,
Be dower'd with those distinctions which alone
The world will value.   Thy true crown is here.

                              [*his hand on his breast.*

Bian. There will I strive to wear it.   But, my lord,
We who live in the world, and for the world
Live chiefly, must our living even so rule
That the world shall not say we live not well.
That we do right, should satisfy ourselves,
And may, we hope, the Almighty; but, for men,
One thing is needed more, — that, doing right,
We seem to do so.   [24] When Your Highness' brother,
The Cardinal Ferdinand, found me at your side

In your sick hour, not knowing we were wed,
His wrath was rous'd.   Even so the hard-judging
world,
Untaught, had frown'd on my best act of duty;
And your own love, that should have rais'd its object,
While blessing, would have robb'd her of her fame.
But for this cause, believe me, dear my lord,
Bianca had been happy unacknowledg'd,
Blest in thy love, content to be thy spouse.
²⁵ Twice happy am I now my fatherland,
Not for my merits, but to honor thee,
Hath given me, for the thousand gifts I owe
Thy matchless love, to make some small return,
Lifting me to thy side more like thy mate.
Thou shalt not find me derogate.   Was I aught
As humble Bonaventuri's wife, I shall
Be ten times more, high-plac'd as Francis' spouse,
Endeavoring so to live, as not to shame
Thy crown, nor that which Venice this day gives.
G. D. But worthier in thyself, than didst thou wear
A crown imperial.   Come; the hour is nigh
Shall tell the world, not me, what thou deserv'st.
Sweet, let us to the robing-room.
                              Bian. Yet first
I have a grace to sue.   Wilt grant it, love?
G. D. What canst thou ask, that Francis will not grant?
Bian. Virginia's mother, twelve long years confin'd
In a dull cloister: set her free, my lord,
And make Virginia happy, and herself.

G. D. Knowest thou what this mother was?   In league
With Ferdinand, using aye in his behoof
The power o'er Cosmo's doting heart she never
Once turn'd to good account, fomenter still
Of discord 'twixt us brothers, and betwixt
Our sire and us, now let her out thou add'st
Another to thy secret foes and mine.
But I have never yet deny'd thee aught.
I will not now, this happy hour. — Virginia!
That day thy hand is given, as thy heart,
To the young lord of Estè, shall thy mother
Revisit the gay world.   Let her beware
So to employ her freedom, that the gift
Be not revok'd.   Nay, kneel not unto me;
Kiss the Grand Duchess' hand.   And bid thy mother
Remember it is she unbars the door,
Not Ferdinand. —

As VIRGINIA *attempts to kneel to* BIANCA, *and kiss
her hand,* BIANCA *draws her to her bosom, and kisses her on
the forehead.*

Ah, gentle love! — Now come.

Exeunt Omnes: the G. D. *and* BIANCA *leading;
behind them the* PATRIARCH *and* CAPELLO; *behind these*
VIRGINIA *and* VITTORIO; *then* PELLEGRINA *and* BENTIVOGLIO;
and finally SENNUCCIO *and* SIGNORA MALOCCORE.

SCENE IV.

A cabinet in the Cardinal de' Medici's palace at Rome.

The CARDINAL, *walking to and fro with signs of
discomposure.* MALOCUORE, *standing.*

Card. Go on.

Mal. I fear your Eminence will lose
Your patience.

    Card. Patience? Hast thou liv'd so long
To wear a beard, and know'st not, what affects
The heart with sudden sorrow, or wounds self-love,
Falls with as passionate impulse on the sense
As news that flatters vanity? By how much
Hate is of more vitality than love,
By so much lend I now the readier ear
In that thy theme offends me. On! go on!

Mal. When the Ambassador, Count Mario Sforza
Of Santa Fiora ——

    Card. Spare me. Need'st thou specify
His titles? Add then, Francis-Mary's minion,
And the Venet —— his Venice woman's tool.

Mal. — Brought back the State's diploma of paternity,
My lord despatch'd the Prince, Don Giovannino,
To thank the Senate.

    Card. A boy but twelve years old!

Apt messenger for such unworthy errand!

                     Mal. Then,
Two of her foremost senators were sent
By Venice, Tiépolo and Michiéli,
To invest her daughter with the parent's rights.
With these ambassadors came ninety nobles,
Both of the sea-girt city and the main;
Such a proud troop as never the Republic
Even in her palmiest fortune sent before.
What but like pomp should answer it? The Court,
The Cabinet, all Florence boasts of great
Or noble, throng'd to meet the imposing train;
Whereof, not least conspicuous for glad zeal,
Shone out my lord, the Prince, Don Pietro.

               Card. [*stopping in his walk.*] Ah!
Say'st thou? 'T is most likely.
In an under but bitter tone, and re-
               suming his walk.] Renegade!
Mal. All the Capello's house and kin were there,
     From the Grand Duchess' sire and uncle down
     To the last gentleman that boasts their blood.
     You had thought them monarchs, conquerors at the
            least.
     Thunder'd the cannon, and the bells rung out
     From every tower, as the Sovereign's guests
     Enter'd the Sovereign's Palace.

                Card. Who?

                   Mal. The House
And kin of Senator Capello.

Card. All?

Mal. To the last gentleman that boasts his blood.

Card. What! Not enough to house the sire and brother?
Must the herd batten where my father fed?

Mal. The sire goes back: but not the brother; who gets
A pension his male issue will inherit, —
His daughter to be dower'd.

     Card. Holy Paul!
This passes all endurance. What! must I,
His father's son, be scanted and put off
In my emergence, that a foreign vermin
May pierce the fisc at will? — What more?

       Mal. 'T is said,
The expenses of the marriage, reckoning all,
From the first mission to the crowning-rite, ﹨
Will make three hundred thousand ducats told.

Card. That while a dearth is pressing sore the land,
And his born subjects pine for simple bread!
O Lord, how long shall the crown'd sons of pride
Abuse their loan'd prerogatives, and make
The sad earth doubt Thy justice?

      Mal. And for one
Not meriting such fortune.

   Card. [*roughly.*] Who is that?
By Heaven, thou! ——
Correcting himself.] Thou mistak'st me much. I meant
Not to impute the fault to her.

   Mal. [*insinuatingly.*] I thought
Your Eminence had hated the Grand Duchess.

Card. Should that prevent my knowledge of her due?
 Her natural gifts of —— To the tale. Proceed.
Mal. " The Ambassadors express'd the Senate's joy,
 That the two cities, henceforth close affin'd ——
Card. Pass all that, — as in time it all will pass.
Mal. And giving to the daughter of the State,
 In the paternal name, a most rare jewel ——
Card. And that. Come to the crowning act.
        Mal. The crown?
Card. Conferr'd this day, I think.
       Mal. About this hour,
 In the Great Hall, most lavishly adorn'd,
 Before the Eight and Forty of the Senate,
 The Grand Duke, on his throne, receives the Duchess,
 Who enters royally array'd, led in
 By the Ambassadors, the whole gorgeous train
 Of Venice nobles following. She takes
 Her seat beside him. The diploma redd,
 And ratify'd, of the conceded honors,
 The diadem is set on her fair brow,
 The nuptial ring is interchang'd anew,
 And, wearing still the crown, the titular Queen,
 Her lord beside her, marches to the Church,
 The heroine of a triumph ——
     Card. [*musingly, and resuming his walk.*
      'T is too late
 Now to regret. I should have lik'd to see it.
Mal. Ay, it will prove a rare burlesque.
       Card. Burlesque!

What mean'st thou? She will well become the crown —
I mean in beauty and in gentle pride.

Musingly.

Methinks I see her now ; her gliding step,
Which scarce was motion, settled to a pace
Of quiet majesty ; her radiant smile,
So proud yet sweet withal, though beaming still,
Yet less diffusive in its light; her eyes ——
Ah, there the ethereal fire, which Earth subdues
With its most tender passions! that soft flame
Which might convince an infidel, for there
The Soul and Heaven give out immortal signs ——

During this spoken meditation, the CARDINAL
has turned his back on MALOCUORE. *Now starting, as if
recollecting himself, he faces suddenly about and sees*
MALOCUORE *watching him intently, who at once
drops his eyes; and the* CARDINAL *resumes.*

Thou seem'st to think it strange I can admire
What all men must admire. 'T is not to love.
Besides this lady still has been for me
Most amiable and wooing.

          Mal. I have thought ——
But pardon me, your Grace. I did forget.

Card. What wouldst thou say? I pardon no reserve.

Mal. Yet, my lord's station, and our Holy Church ——

Card. Is 't that? Were not the Apostles flesh and blood?
Thou 'dst speak, I see, of me and of Bianca.

What hast thou seen? Speak out! Thou hast thought
    — thou saidst —

Mal. I have thought at times, my lord, your brother's spouse
Measur'd your fair proportions with an eye
Of capable relish. The Grand Duke is comely;
    But my lord Cardinal's youth and finer features ——

Card. Thou art a serpent. Think'st thou I am Adam?
I hanker not for the Forbidden Fruit.
Dream'st thou I do?

         Mal. My lord would not, I see,
Admit me to his confidence.

            Card. Because
I have no secret. The Venetian is
My brother's spouse. That he has made this choice
Displeases me, because it wrongs our House,
And mars its influence with foreign Courts.
Therefore I view her with such evil will
As may beseem a Christian and a prince
Of Holy Church. I do admire her too, —
Esteem her worthy even of a crown,
Were that not what it is. But love her! — I
Forgive thee, Malocuore. We will talk
Further anon. [*Exit Malocuor.*

The Cardinal *looks after him a moment with an expression*
of triumph and disdain.

         Make *thee* my confidant! —
I will, so far as suits me; not so far

As make thee, dog! my master. No, let fools
Unlock their hearts to knaves. The key to mine
Lies only in my keeping, and shall ever. —
And to betray a love I shame to own
Even to myself! Not that Bianca is
My brother's spouse. [27] My father lov'd my sister:
And his last wife methinks was fond of me.
And but I was too young, perhaps in turn
I had lov'd her too. I put her though to use.
She was my reservoir; I drew from her
The gold Francesco could not, and for which
He hated me. But I should shame to own
I love his Favorite's widow, when for like love
I scorn him, as I hate him doubly too,
If aught indeed can double hate like mine.
[28] And her too I shall use — if not for pleasure,
For profit. What imply those words that came,
Wrapp'd with the picture I had pray'd to have?

> *Takes, from a drawer of an open
> writing-table, a miniature, incased, and a
> letter. Opening the latter he appears to read
> in it. Then:*

[29] *She cannot live without me ?* [pause.

        — *Lives in me ?* [pause.

Is it the simple passion of her nature
Lends her these phrases; for her way is loving
And tender unto all; or? —— We shall see.
This coronation over —— Would the crown

Were fire to burn her temples, though I would
So gladly feel them beat against my heart!
This over, she shall see me at her wish. [*pause.*
[20] No, it were better first to write. I will —
Will test her kindness. She shall use her hold
On my weak brother's heart to unlock his treasure.
I need fresh means. His hand, which never shuts
When a show 's promis'd or an artist sues,
Closes, perhaps instinctively, to me,
As if he felt his gold would prop the lever
That shakes his throne.   Ah ! when that throne shall crumble
To pieces at my touch, to be rebuilt
For a more resolute ruler; when the wrong
Which nature did me when she made him first,
Though I was meant for government —— As yet
See I but darkly what my soul bids do
To rectify this wrong ; but what I do
Shall be so done 't will not need doing over.
When I throw off this purple which I hate ——
But where wilt then *thou* be ? [*gazing on the miniature.*
                         Or being, *what*,
What wilt thou then be?— Mine thou shalt be,
    or ! ——
I hate thee as I love thee [*kissing passionately the glass.*]:
    't seemeth now,
As I gaze on that proud, yet winning smile,
Which woos yet mocks me, seems it to me now,
As I could kiss and choke thee at one breath.

Accurs'd enchantress! Such my tools have made
The credulous crowd believe thee. And thou art!
Thou art! But thy enchantments are all here.

*Gazing on the miniature a moment, he
closes the case, and walks up to the writing-table, to replace it,
and Scene closes.*

·

♦

SCENE V.

Florence. The Great Hall in the Pitti Palace.

The GRAND DUKE, *wearing the grand-ducal crown
and robes, and seated on his throne, surrounded by the Senate
of Forty-eight, and the Magistrates in a semicircle on
either side. Within the crescent, on his right,* DON PIETRO, *the*
DUKE OF BRACCIANO, DON CÆSAR D' ESTE, ARCH-
BISHOP OF PISA, ABBIOSO, *&c. On the left* DONNA VIRGINIA,
PELLEGRINA, SIGNORA MALOCUORE *and other ladies.*

*The Hall, magnificently draped, is hung with banners, &c.,
and the whole Court is in sumptuously festal and
solemn array.
On either side a line of soldiery extending up to the
throne, with banners of arms, &c., among
which those of Venice are
conspicuous.*

*A grand burst of music,
and Enter*

in royal robes, her train borne up by two Pages, BIANCA
conducted by the two Venetian AMBASSADORS,
and followed immediately by BARTHOLOMEW CAPELLO *and the*
PATRIARCH, *and en suite by* VITTORIO, *and a long train
of Venetian nobles gorgeously apparelled.*

G. D. [*descending the steps before his throne.*
Our well-belov'd, right royal Duchess!   Sit
Bodily at our hand, who in our heart
In spirit art ever thron'd. [*Places her on the throne and
sits beside her.*
Rever'd Capello!
Our lady's noble father; thou, grave Patriarch,
Her honor'd uncle and ours; be seated near.
[*They take their places on his right.*
Our sometime Auditor, most Reverend Sire
In God, Archbishop Antony of Pisa,
Read the diploma of St. Mark's adoption,
For which cause sit we here.

Archb. [*reading.*

In the high name
Of the august Republic, we the Doge
And joint Pregadi, wishing to attest
Our deep sense of the many and rare virtues
Which render worthy of the highest fortune
Blanche, daughter of the Senator Capello,
Whom the Great Duke of Tuscany has wed,
And to do honor to the Great Duke's self,
Adopt her as the daughter of the State,
Conceding unto her the rank and title
Of Queen of Cyprus, with all high prerogatives
And honors which to the adoptive parent
Of right belong.

G. D. Speak ye, the Ambassadors
Of Venice, Excellent Signori Tiepolo
And Michïeli, is that your Senate's voice?
Tiep. It is.
Mich. We ratify it, and pronounce
By virtue of our warrant, in the name
Of Holy Mark, the Lady Blanche Capello
True and legitimate Child of the Republic.
Tiep. In whose high name we place this royal crown
On her fair brows.

> *The* AMBASSADORS *crown her,* — BIANCA
> *advancing and standing up.*

Both. } Long live the Queen Bianca!

Venetian }
Nobles. } Live Queen Bianca!

The Guards, presenting arms, and their stand-
ard-bearers waving all the banners, join in the
cry. A burst of music.

Patriarch. 'T is the Senate's wish
Of Venice, and the Great Duke lends consent,
The high espousals solemniz'd before
Between His Highness and the Lady Blanche,
Born daughter of Bartholomew Capello,
Should by His Highness this day be renew'd
With the Queen, daughter of St. Mark. Advance,
Ambassadors, and give away the bride.

The Nuptial ring is exchanged
in the customary form, and the PATRIARCH, *spreading*
his hands over the pair, appears to repeat the
prayers and benediction. Then a'oud:

Heaven on these nuptials shower perennial joy;
And give the fair engrafted plant to glad
With long fecundity the sovereign stock;
So after ages, happy in its shade,
May bless, as I do now, the parent seed!
G. D. Now to the Church, to offer thanks to God.
And meetly close this high auspicious day.

The Characters and other persons
form in procession, which passes down and from the scene
in the following order :
PATRIARCH OF AQUILEIA *and* ARCHBISHOP OF PISA.
BIANCA, *with the crown on her head, led by the* GRAND DUKE,
and having her train borne up by the SIGNORA MALOCUOR
and another LADY OF THE COURT, — *the Gr. Duke's train*
borne by two PAGES.   *Then* DON PIETRO, *with* BAR-
THOLOMEW CAPELLO; DONNA VIRGINIA *with* DON CÆSAR
D' ESTE; *the* DUKE OF BRACCIANO *with* VITTORIO; PEL-
LEGRINA *with* BENTIVOGLIO ; SENNUCCIO
and ABBIOSO; SENATE.
Then the train of VENETIAN NOBLES ; *then the* INFERIOR
MAGISTRATES; *and finally the* GUARD, *which have*
presented arms as the procession passes between
the lines.   Music playing throughout, until

the Drop falls.

Act the Fifth

Scene I.   A room in the Grand Duchess's Apartment.

Bianca.   Cardinal.

Card. Nay, it is so.   Your modesty disowns
Your kindness' due.   I know my brother's heart:
One may wring aught from it but gold.
                    Bian. My lord,
You do him wrong.   A freer hand or heart
Can boast no monarch: few so free.
                    Card. Well, well;
I will not argue — not with you.   Once more,
A thousand thanks.   I would I could believe
I ow'd your kindness to a dearer feeling.
Bian. Than what, my lord?
                    Card. Than that which you profess.
Oft in your letters you have call'd me dear;
And when you bade me hasten from dead Rome
To give new life to Florence and to you,
It was with such a magic of sweet words
As lent even to your picture sweeter charms.
May I believe them real?
                    Bian. My poor words?
O yes!   Indeed, save dear Virginia only,

Who of my lord's near blood can be to me
That which your Highness' talents, winning way,
And suavity of speech have render'd you?
Card. And is that all?   Alas! your pictur'd lips
Give back no colder answer.
                              Bian. Does your Grace
Then question them?   When, at your prayer, I sent
My poor resemblance, pleas'd to think you held
In some regard your brother's wife, I sent
Truly my heart with it.   Did your Grace in turn
Give truly yours?
                    Card. So truly, and so wholly,
I come to seek it.   Give me back my own.
Or satisfy the sweet yet painful void
That leaves my breast no respite.
                              Bian. My lord Cardinal!
This language in a Churchman ——
                         Card. Seems it strange?
Has not a Churchman senses?   Are they proof
To that delicious sickness whose contagion
Seizes the spirits of all other men?
Bian. My lord! my lord!   Either yourself are mad,
Or you think me so.   If you not remember
What your position calls for, at the least
Forget not what belongs to mine.   [*Turns to go.*
                         Card. Yet stay!
Beauteous Bianca! hear me yet one word.
Bian. My lord, a thousand — in another tone,
And of another import.

Card. 'T is to say,
You disavow the affection you have own'd,
And bid me to forget what I have learn'd.

Bian. It is to say, I bid your Grace remember
I proffer'd but a sisterly regard;
Which still is yours, if you will take it fairly;
But, to pervert it to a guilty thought,
Is to charge *me* with folly, and yourself.

Card. Why guilty? You have said, my speech and ways
Won from you liking. Was 't in nature then,
I should not yield the body of my soul
Captive to beauty, wit, and grace like thine?
That magic which entrances all the world
That come within its circle, which has wrapt
My eldest brother for so many years
In such infatuate passion that fools say
Thou usest philters, shall it have no spell
For a more sympathetic spirit like mine?
Yes! fairest of all ——

Bian. [*who has looked steadily on him, throughout his appeal,
with a scorn gradually increasing.*
Must I understand
By this, your Eminence would make love to me?

Card. Ah, look not thus! though even scorn shows beau-
tiful
In that angelic face. Saints look not down
On their poor worshipers with gleaming eyes:
And I am such; I love not, but adore.
Thou art a Gorgon now; but not the terror

Of those haught looks can frown me into stone;
For my blood boils with passion.

Bianca moves to touch a hand-bell.] Yet fear not!
Ring not! I have but words: words which shall out,
Though, could I now go back, I would not breathe
    them.
Bianca, I adore thee; with a passion
Which makes the love of even my brother tame.
I am more young than he, my heart less worn.
Look on me, and compare us. Is he comelier?
Has he? ———

    Bian. My lord, is this mere gallantry?
Or comes it truly from your inmost soul?
Card. From the hot heart of my impassion'd spirit.
I swear it by my habit, by the Church,
By the high God in Heaven, and what for me
Has all of Heaven in one thought — thyself!
I love thee with a passion! ———
                Bian. Hear me then.
Were I so meanly, loathsomely ingrate,
As to forget all good I owe my lord;
Could I be, what as yet I ne'er have been,
So intemperate of blood as at one time
To love two men; could I so far forget
My duty unto God and unto man,
As, with a double adultery, to yield
My body to my lord's own brother; still,
Still would I shrink, as from the touch of plague,
From taint by such a traitor — traitor, ay! [31]

Traitor unto thy God, thy Church, thy brother!
The hooded snake, which bites even unassail'd,
Shall be as welcome to my breast as thou!
   She takes up the bell; but at the moment

Enter VIRGINIA.

O my Virginia! thou art come in time.
Card. [*who at first springs towards Bianca, as though he
   would strangle her, turning about, and with clenched
   hands, mutters :*
Death! 'I should sink to this!* [*Exit.*
               Virg. What troubles thee,
Sweet sister? Thine eyes blaze, albeit thy cheek
Is fearful-pale.
     Bian. The Cardinal and I
Have had high words. I do repent me much
I strove to reconcile my lord and him.
But thou look'st sad too. Is it all for me?
Virg. Alas! My mother! They have taken her back
To her old cloister. Dare I pray once more
Thy influence with my lord and brother?
                 Bian. I fear
'T will be in vain. Yet, for thy gentle sake,
I will essay. And happily now comes
The Duke. Thou wilt not go?
             Virg. 'T is best.
What could my tears with him, if thy prayer fail?
                        [*Exit.*

Enter GRAND DUKE.

G. D. Virginia? Flies she me? Thy darling friend
Should feel her presence here is joy to me.
Bian. She had a grace to ask, and, dear my lord,
Would trust my pleading rather than her own.
G. D. Knowing I could refuse thee nothing, ha?
Bian. My lord is ever gracious; but this quest
I fear will try him. 'T is her mother's cause.
G. D. Pray, do not plead for her. I have no heart
To say thee nay. But now —— Dost thou remember,
I gave Virginia warning that her mother
Must not abuse her freedom? Yet her home
Was made the haunt of traitors, who paid court
And offer'd mock condolence to the widow,
That they might shame their Sovereign, teaching men
To call me tyrant and set her in honor
Above my own thron'd Duchess. Chief of these
Were my born brothers; and of these the chief
Was Ferdinand. Thou changest hue! I mark'd,
On coming in, thy forehead was o'erclouded,
And thy pal'd cheeks show'd traces of a storm.
What has befallen?
                    Bian. What never must again.
I have borne, my lord, from the o'erweening prelate,
What makes me sorry you are not still foes.
G. D. Ha! Has the ungrateful traitor dar'd renew
His old despite?
                    Bian. It were not wise, my lord,

Even were it noble, to accuse the absent;
Nor, speaking to my sovereign and my spouse,
Can I forget the reverence due his blood;
But this in brief — and it is much to say:
The Cardinal-Prince in me sees but the widow
Of Bonaventuri, in himself the son
Of Cosmo.

    G. D. The old devil of his nature;
A rampant arrogance that gets the better
Even of his practis'd craft. It shall be tam'd.
His visit over, let this ill-starr'd union
Be never more renew'd. He but abuses
My trust, as thy sweet nature. Florence is full
Of plots and treason of his foul engendering,
Hatch'd into life and foster'd by the means
I lent him at thy instance. Malocuor
Begins to give me doubts; and Pietro falls
Visibly once more in the traitorous mesh.
Hast thou not mark'd this?

                Bian. No, my lord: till now
I doubted not the Cardinal was restor'd
To godlier feelings.

    G. D. Such he never knew.
And Pietro is the fool of his own passions,
Which Ferdinand plays with, with a master hand,
For his ambitious aims. — Yet be to both,
Until the banquet and the hunt are over
Which end this luckless visit, gracious still.

Bian. Still, as befits me ever to our guests

And to thy brothers.   But to seem again
That which I was, when, deeming I had won
Ilis heart in turn, I held the Cardinal dear,
That can I not.

       G. D. And that I would not have.
Be, as Heaven made thee, open as the day,
And leave to those, whose thoughts bear not the light,
To mask their visages. — But I am come,
Not to condole with thee, nor yet to praise thee,
But have thy sentence on the gem they are adding
To our art-treasures, for whose wasteless wealth,
Thus gather'd, coming time shall laud my name.

Bian. The new-found statue?

       G. D. 'T is now clean'd, and shows
A prodigy of beauty, scarcely flaw'd.
How Benvenuto's eyes had glisten'd over
Its grand yet fine proportions! — Come, love, come!

Bian. O my dear lord, I should but mar your pleasure.
Hold me excus'd.   A weight is on my soul
I cannot lift; a presage of dire evil.
The shape I see not, but the thing is there.

G. D. It is a shade then.   Wears it Ferdinand's hat?

Bian. [gravely.

I have said what Ferdinand never will forgive.

G. D. And thus that gentle heart is made uneasy,

               [folding his arms about her.

Sorrowing for wounds it has made another bear,
Albeit in self-defence.

       Bian. That is not all.

The Cardinal's face was black with gather'd hate.

G. D. He is a serpent. Fear not therefore thou.
The cygnet is beneath the parent's wing.

[*pressing her closer.*

Can the snake reach it? Fie, thou timid swan!
Summon thy ladies, and be with me straight.

Kisses her hand, and Exit.

Bian. But with a heart thy dear love cannot lighten.
Would it were morrow and the Cardinal gone!

Moving to the table, lifts the hand-bell, as to ring it;

and Scene changes to

Scene II.

A room in Malocuore's house.

Malocuor
*walking slowly, with an air of deep meditation,
his hand on his chin.*

Enter
Signora Malocuore — *her face radiant with triumph.*

Sign. What wilt thou give me for the news I bring?
Mal. [*gazing at her for a moment sharply.*
'T is something fatal; something —— Thou shalt have
A carcanet of diamonds, bring'st thou such
As shall destroy the Duchess, and perhaps ——
       [*checking himself.*
I will not tell thee that.
    Sign. Perchance I know.
Thou plottest for the ruin — it may be
The murder of thy lord, to place the Card ——
Mal. [*in alarm and threateningly.*
Wilt hold thy wicked tongue? How know'st thou?
Walls
Thick as our own have ears.
    Sign. That know I well:

Our mistress's for instance.

           Mal. Ha! —   Speak out.

But whisper.   'T is? ——

       Sign. [*pausing — then slowly.*

        The Cardinal loves Bianca.

Mal. [*peevishly.*

   That is old news for me.

         Sign. But not so old,

The Cardinal has avow'd his passion, and been ——

Mal. [*eagerly interrupting.*

Say but rejected, thou hast made us both.

Sign. Rejected; with such virulence of scorn,

But that I heard, I had not thought her mouth

Could breathe such accents.

       Mal. [*rapturously.*] This is Heaven!

              Sign. Hell rather.

Mal. Ay, Hell for them; but a brave Heaven to me.

     Two slow taps heard at the door.

Go now; there comes, and in the nick of time,

One I must deal with.

       Sign. [*going.*] Have a care!

           Mal. Be sure. [*Exit Sign.*

             by another door.

Now, no more doubt! [*exultingly.*] 'T is ripe! ——

                 Come in.

        Enter

   by the first door, MASNADIERE.

Masnad. Your Excellence has order'd ——

>   *Mal.* [*bringing him forward.*
>   Come this way.

And speak more low. — Thou hast a nimble tongue
As well as poniard. Knowest thou a man
Thy mate therein ?

>   *Masnad.* Your Excellence, I do.

Mal. Canst thou malign a person of high rank
Even in his very teeth ? and foil his thrusts,
If he push questions home ?   .

>   *Masnad.* I have foil'd home-thrusts
Of sharper stuff than words, and done more hurt
To persons of high rank than with my tongue.

Mal. Know'st thou the tavern of the Golden Lilies ?
Betake thee thither then —— Soft ! I must see
This mate of thine. Go, bring him hither straight.
But not that way. I'll show thee now a room,
Where I can teach you two and not a soul
Know of the lesson. There a secret stair
Leads to a little garden-gate, whereby
Thou 'lt bring thy fellow. Follow. Softly ! So.

>   *Leads off, on tiptoe, and with finger on lip,*
>   MASNADIERE *by a small door to the*
>   *further part of the scene.*

SCENE III.

A room in the Cardinal's Apartment at the Pitti.

CARDINAL. DON PIETRO.

Don P. I know not that. If, the last time, 't was feign'd,
Why feign'd she not the birth too? Why resort
To visceral pangs, at peril of her life,
To end a pregnancy, which, if 't were shamm'd,
She would have clos'd by simulated travail
And a supposititious offspring.
                    Card. Why?
Because she knew I had set a watch on her.
Don P. If she knew that, she could have chang'd her
   creatures,
  And so avoided it, did she deceive.
'T were harder for her to o'erreach in this
Her lord than thee. Now, by the gods! I think
'T was poison given her to prevent a birth.
Card. Thou dost not hint I gave it?
                  Don P. Faith! our sire
Was thought a subtle poison-mixer: Strozzi,
Who had tried the like on him, had cause to dread him.

Thou hast, I know, his art.   Say, thou dost use it;
That is thine own affair.
                    Card. Art thou gone mad?
Dost thou forget my habit and my place?
Don P. No, I remember priests may do for God
What laïcs do for Satan.   How much more
A *prince* of Holy Church!
                    Card. A scurril jest;
Which I might take for earnest, were 't my will.
But for thy sake, my brother, I can bear,
With the Lord's grace, even that.
                    Don P. [*scornfully.*] For mine?
                    Card. Thine only.
Don P. Hark!   I 'm thy junior, Ferdinand; but no babe,
To bite on coral.
                    Card. And I hold thee none.
Let the witch foist on her besotted lord
Some peasant or strumpet's bantling, who shall climb
Our father's throne, what is my loss?   Hurt pride.
The purple bars me from succession; but thou,
Wounded in honor, art shut out from the crown,
Which is thy natural right, failing Francis' heirs.
More, thou art wrong'd in the present: our sire's wealth
Must make the nest warm for the cuckoo's brood.
What!   Thou art touch'd at last?   Why so! why so!
'T was well reminded.   Wilt thou not awake?
Promise me thou wilt marry, dear Pietro!
'T is the sole hope for Florence and for me,

Who count our House's honor next to God's.

Don P. Why press that point?   'T is time when I succeed.

Card. And shouldst thou die?   What hope then for our
    House?
Shall this pernicious harlot's purchas'd seed
Mount to my father's heritage?   Perish rather
She and her prematurely dotard spouse
By one quick blow together!
                    Don P. Sayest thou, brother?
How happens it that thou, who wast but now
In amity with the Duchess, art fallen out?

Card. Because but now she has wrong'd me with sharp
    insult,
As lately thee.   Thou lov'st her not?
                    Don P. Why no.
She might have had my Spaniard at the Court.[33]
But that the girl was not made welcome, is that
A cause to foul her Highness with gross names?
Troth! I believe I honor her in heart
The more she did not.
                    Card. So not I!   It was
The rankest hypocrisy.   The harlot soul
Loves most the form of chastity.   Out upon
These whited sepulchres!   The flowers that prank
Their outward wall draw beauty from corruption,
And lade the churchyard air with scents that bring
To wise minds thoughts of rottenness.
                    Don P. My mind

Is dull then as my eyes. I see but beauty
And smell but sweetness in Bianca. Yet,
God wot, I love her not.
     Card. Well. To the point.
I have certain cause to think the fresh maternity
Our Duchess threatens is but assum'd. Wilt thou
Be diligent as I to thwart her aims?

Don. P. Why yes, so far.
     Card. 'T is for thy good, not mine.
The honor of our House, there, there alone,
I vie with thee in interest. We will talk
Further of this. Meantime, spread thou by stealth,
But largely, what I have told thee. Thou mayst
 safely.
Think of our father's throne, and of his wealth
Squander'd on bastards. With that spur, devise;
And make her fame as odious as thou canst.

Don P. I will think on 't; but, 'sooth! I like it not.
'T were manlier far to poison her outright.
       [*Exit Don P.*

Card. And would she were! to save thy brains the pain,
 Thou shallow libertine! — and me perhaps
 The odium of the deed. — I could not prick
 Thy honor to the leap; I touch'd thy purse.
 Well — there thou art not far wrong. — But who
  had thought
 I could so blind thee! *Thou* succeed! *Thy* heirs!
 The purple bar my natural rights! A word,

The Pope gives dispensation; [34] and my vows
And habit alike are cobwebs. They shall mesh
Thee as some bigger flies. Then break thou through,
If thou have power!

Enter MALOCUORE.

Ha, Malocuor! — Come forward. —
Why art thou dull? Why, man! the sun looks bright
That dawns upon our fortune. Saidst thou not
The people famine-stricken were astir,
Rous'd by the Duke's exactions? that the nobles,
Fir'd by the sequestration of the goods
Of the conspiring twenty of their order,
Are disaffected? (little do they think
'T was of my prompting!) and Camilla's lot
Is made to appear a grievous wrong? Hear now : —
The Queen of France has charg'd — thou know'st well
    why —
Troilo Orsini's murder on thy master,
Who is as innocent of his death as thou.
St. Mark's portentous star is on the wane.
Thou shak'st the head! Why, what is this?
                                        Mal. My lord —
Could I dare speak ——
                    Card. Thou mayst say what thou wilt.
Hast thou not heard I pardon no reserve?
Mal. A strange report is running through the town,

The Cardinal-Prince — forgive, your Grace! — made
love
Openly to his brother's spouse, and was ——
Card. 'T is false as Hell! a devilish juggling lie!
But what if it were true? Say on.
                              Mal. And was ——
Instantly and with scorn rejected.
                              Card. Death!
Where gott'st thou that? Where? Quickly! Stam-
mer not!
Or! ——
    Mal. Everywhere and anywhere. Aloud
In the open marketplaces, in the taverns,
'T is told with laughter. Men exalt the Duchess
As a Penelope, and deride your Grace.
Card. Villain! thou liest!
                              Mal. Give me then to death.
But if I do not? ——
                    Card. Then shall die the inventor.
Mal. That is the Duchess' self. She told her ladies;
And, ere you might count ten, ——
                              Card. O, that her neck
Were 'twixt these fingers! — But I 'll not believe it!
Thou art impos'd on — or imposest. I will
Have instant proofs! Dost hear me? instant proofs!
Proofs, dost thou hear me! proofs, I say!
                              Mal. And shall.
Card. But on the instant! I will have no stop.

Mal. Will your Grace venture then to come with me?

Card. To bring the source of that infernal slander
　　Home to that — woman?　Whither not?　To Hell,
　　Must I there seek it.

　　　　　　　Mal. Could your Grace procure
A close disguise.

　　　　　Card. At once.

　　　　　　　　Mal. [*turning to go.*
　　　　　　　I will be back
Similarly metamorphos'd —

　　　　　　Card. In five minutes.
Go.　I will have this proof, or — 'ware thy soul!

　　　　　　　　　　　　　　　　[*Exit.*

　　MALOCUOR, *looking after him with a sinister smile,*
　　　raises his hand exultingly, and Exit by the
　　　　　door where he had entered.

Scene IV.

A large public room in the Tavern of the Golden Lilies. Various groups of common men, artisans, etc., with soldiers intermixed, drinking at separate tables. At a table in the foreground, standing by itself,

MASNADIERE *and* SCHERANO.

Scher. Who is this man of rank he is to bring?

Masnad. I know not, I; and care as little. Most like,
     The Cardinal's self.

                    Scher. That is a daring thought.
     How should it stead him, what we have to say?

Masnad. Much, an' thou weigh'st the matter. Was't not
     thou,
     With Malandrino and myself, wast sent,
     To stir the people, when our Lady's brother,
     Vittorio, had displac'd the favorite lords,
     Pandolfo of the Bardi, Mario Sforza,
     And Jacopo Salviati, the Duke's cousin?
     Holp we not make the imposts too weigh heavier
     In popular estimation by our talk?
     Was thy purse empty, when the city rung
     With rumors of great crimes most like our own,
     Imputed to the Grand Duke's self, with some,
     Dyed deeper with a diabolical craft,

Wrought by the Duchess and a Jewish hag
Confederate in her sorceries, acts to make
Even our flesh'd senses shudder ? [36]

      Scher. With disgust.

Pah! I recall 't.   I was asham'd to find
Men, that had brains, so credulous.

      Masnad. Why! Thou shouldst
Rather have blush'd to wonder.   Lies as gross
I have read in history, and suppose these too
Will find some godly chronicler one day,
With fools to credit him.   For, mark you! men
Love nothing better than a good round lie
That, blackening others, makes themselves more white
In their own fancies; and a monstrous tale
Has marvelous attraction for some ears
Which shut at simple facts.   Cry thou, Amen!
So fellows like thee and me get their deserts
With royal company in bad renown.
Well now, I say, who fee'd our tongues for this?
Who but the Signor Malocuor?   And where
Got he the ducats?   Not from Francis-Mary;
Nor from Don Pietro.   Seest thou, ha?

      Scher. I see:
The Red-Cap 's hawking at his brother's crown.
But wherefore changes Malocuor his game,
Praising the Duchess? —

    Masnad. And reviling him?
I know not.   But, thou seest, the tale not now
Is for the common ear: the Cardinal's own

Haply is meant. Perchance to lash his purpose
To some bold leap.
          Scher. Brave! That may need our help.
Masnad. But will not•get it — not mine — if, as I think,
It vault too high.
          Scher. Thou mean'st?
              Masnad. At the Grand Duchess,
Or the Grand Duke himself.
             Scher. By Bacchus! no!
That were to swallow coals. 'T is desperate-bold
As 't is: our talk will drive the Cardinal wild.
Masnad. Not before us. But after! ——
              Scher. Then look sharp;
Your steed may throw you, Signor Malocuor!

       Enter, in disguise,
     CARDINAL *and* MALOCUORE.

Masnad. Hush! 't is our men. Play well now.
              Mal. [*low.*] Have a care,
My gracious lord! [*Aloud, in an assumed voice.*
          Shall we go higher up?
Or choose our table here?
           Card. [*also assumed voice.*
         Here is as well.
Mal. Have you room, friends?
        Masnad. At your good service. Sit.
Mal. If we not interrupt your converse. [*Card. and Mal. sit.*
       Masnad. No.

We prate but idly, and of public things.

Mal. [*to a waiter, who has approached them.*

    Monte Pulciano. —

               To Masnad.] We are strangers here.

Masnad. From Lucca?

         Mal. Ay. You Florentines detect

Lightly our accent.

         Masnad. 'T is not strongly mark'd.

Mal. Sir, you are complaisant.

Waiter brings wine and glasses, is paid and retires.

             Please ye to partake

Of our poor beverage. [*filling for all.*

         Masnad. Drink we to the health ——

Scher. Of the Grand Duchess, foremost of all ladies!

       They all rise — CARDINAL *reluctantly ;*

who coughs and sets down his glass untasted.

Mal. With all my heart.

         Masnad. Your friend admires not much

Our mistress.

       Mal. Ay, but better loves the Church.

Scher. Perhaps another toast ——

         Card. Nay, that was well:

But I drink rarely.

       Scher. And speak seldom.

             Card. How!

            [*Mal. pushes him secrefly.*

Mal. He is taciturn — yet choleric too. What news?

Is there aught stirring?

         Masnad. You are strange indeed!

Stirring? All Florence is astir.

      Mal. With what?

Masnad. The Cardinal's amours.

      Mal. [*making again a sign to Card.*

      to restrain himself.

      Cardinal who?

      Scher. His Grace,

The Cardinal de' Medici, our Sovereign's brother.

Mal. [*again touching the Card. who betrays discomposure.*

  Sure, they malign him. Who the happy fair?

Scher. Happy? Not much of that! He was rebuff'd.

Masnad. The dame — what think ye, sirs — especially you

Who love the Church? — was his own brother's spouse,

Our lady Duchess!

      Card. [*starting up, and in his natural voice.*

      That is false!

      Masnad. [*starting up too, and*

      half-drawing his dagger.

      By Heaven!

Mal. [*affecting to restrain him.*

  You have no cause; my comrade's zeal ——

      Card. [*with composure and in his assumed voice.*

      Your pardon.

Not your report I question'd, but the tale;

Which, for the love I bear our Holy Church,

      [*crossing himself.*

I say again, is falsehood black as Hell.

Masnad. 'T is well. But give me leave to tell you, brother,

If you come here to battle for the Church

With all who argue her of filthy sin,
You should provide yourself a score of lives.
Card. That is my risk. — But whence had you this story?
Masnad. Whence? Whence you will? 'T is common as
    church-psalms.
    Shall I call hither some of yonder groups,
    To laugh you into faith? Else, an' you list,
    Here is my fellow had the tale direct.
Scher. Ay, from Bettina. She 's to me, you wot,
    Much as your Cardinal would, but could not have,
    To him our Duchess. Now Bettina's mistress
    Is aunt of Count Ulysses Bentivoglio,
    Whose spouse, the Duchess' daughter, Pellegrina,
    Taught by her mother, told it unto her.
  Mal. It is enough.
        Card. To prove the rumor, not its truth.
Scher. What take you then our Cardinal to be?
    A saint in sackcloth? or Saint Dominic?
    Body of Bacchus! 't is a gallant prince,
    Young, handsome —— Let me see. [*peering in*
                      Card.'s face.
                Why, as I live!
    He 's not unlike yourself, though finer far,
    And some years younger, and, by right of blood,
    Adorer of fair ladies.
        Card. [*rising — to Mal.*
        Let us go.
Mal. [*rising.*] Good morning, gentlemen.
             Masnad. Good morning, both.

Scher. [*to Card., who has turned.*

And, brother, in your prayers remember me.

[*Exeunt Card. and Mal.*

Was 't not well play'd?

Masnad. God's faith! 't was all put home.

Not Cini's surgery [37] will heal those wounds.

Scher. How he reneg'd! Now, as a soldier true,

Holdst thou him guilty?

Masnad. Guilty, by this hilt!

Is Malocuor stark mad, without some base

To build such fabric? At a touch 't would fall

And crush him into atoms.

Scher. Precious prelate!

This comes of giving princes to the Church.

Masnad. — Without a true vocation. See thou now!

We both wax godly.

Scher. Right enough, when rogues

Usurp the purple.

Masnad. Bravo, my Scherano!

When I am Pope, look thou art made Archbishop.

Scher. I will not covet then my neighbor's wife.

Masnad. Brave! But forget not, Eminence, our Cardinal

But took his brother's place, young Don Giovanni,

Whom swart Garzía stabb'd.

Scher. Whose fault was that?

Masnad. Why Cosmo's. But they are all a cursed race.

Scher. So Isabella cried. And I, Amen!

Would we were rid of all your serpent brood!

Masnad. Then thou criedst evil. Take their slime away,

The grass would grow too green for thee and me.
Set Florence free again, and sift the laws
The bloody Spaniard model'd for our soil,
Would six score annual murders feed us fat ?
Stablish right rule, the first stroke of its wand
Would sweep us clean away, with all our webs,
Which we have spun in palaces.   Where then
The twice two hundred of our valiant corps,
Whose lightning, hurtled by the lion's cub,
Men call the Cardinal Farnese's son,
Pietro Leoncillo da Spoleti,
Frightens the confines with its errant blaze, — [38]
Where shall they forage, then ?   And all the bands
High barons and proud princes of the Church
Pay or connive at for their private ends ?
Useless, they shrink, and vanish by degrees.
The rights of nature, which our foes call rapine,
And the strong arm are put in sequestration,
Bound by the moral fetters of the weak.
Money must then be earn'd by vulgar toil ;
And men of mettle, coop'd like barnyard birds,
No more like falcons winnow the free air
With wings unclipp'd and dip their beaks in blood.
Law helps the coward and makes strong the weak. —
When then, for that his man's-heart durst aspire
To free Italia from a bestial yoke,
They put wise Machiavelli to the rack,[39]
They did good service to us sons of fortune ;

For which let us be thankful.   Live the Medici!

         [Drinks.

Scher. Amen! if they 're our Providence.   But one,

His spouse at least, will not be better long

For thy mock loyalty, see I clearly through

Our patron's masquerade.

       Masnad. Or haply both.

So, Good night, Signor Malocuor!

         Scher. How so?

Masnad. Thinkst thou, his height once clomb, your crafty

  Cardinal

Will let the ladder stand to mark his way?

Push'd down, the steps are broken, or hid, rest sure.

Scher. In cell or coffin then, rot unbewail'd,

Thou worst as meanest villain of us all!

Masnad. That is wish'd well.   And so I drink, Amen!

         [Drinks.

    They pass up the stage

  to mingle with the other groups, and

     Scene closes.

Scene V.

Same as Scene III.

Enter precipitately, the Cardinal *followed by* Malocuore,
both still wearing their disguise.

Card. [*dashing down his hat and throwing off passionately
his coarse mantle.*

Hell's hottest fires on her treacherous soul!
Would I could slay her inch by inch, and make,
For her, a twelvemonth's agony of death!
Mal. [*helping to divest him.*

That were not easy. And your Highness' hopes
Would only be twelve useless months delay'd.
At once, and by a single blow, 't were best.
Card. Do it at once, then!
          Mal. Has your Grace forgot?
There is another life.
          Card. What mean'st thou?
                    Mal. Dies
The sorceress on the instant, with her dies
Your great revenge. But live to better hope
Your glorious aspirations and your rights?
          *He pauses a moment, looking intently
on the* Cardinal, *who motions him to proceed.*

Your royal brother weds again; and then ——

[*pauses again.*

Card. Devil!

Mal. Or saint, even as it suits my lord.

But devil would stand him now in better stead.

Card. Be thou the devil, then. But let thy tongue

Speak out thy damnable purpose in few words.

Or, if thou canst, hint what is neither fit

For thee to utter nor for me to hear. [*Walks away.*

Mal. Has your Grace much remaining of the sum

The Duchess strove so hard that you might get ?

Card. [*turning quickly.*

Serpent! thou stingest. —— Twice fifteen thousand

went, —

Thou hadst the distribution, and shouldst know,—

To gain new friends, and to secure the old.

Mal. Would twice five thousand ducats be too much,

To help your Highness to the throne of Florence

And your most just revenge ?

     Card. Take ten times that :

And ten times more, if needful: what thou wilt.

Mal. Hypothecations on the royal fisc ?

No; ten suffice. — There is a white confection,

A tremulous jelly made of sweeten'd milk,

And scented with the water of the rose.

Of this the royal pair are strangely fond.

At the grand banquet, meant to usher in

That purpos'd chase which never shall take place,

Eschew this viand. Its taste engenders thirst,

Which might prove fatal.   On the morrow, men
Shall hail your Highness Sovereign Duke in Florence.
                    [*Exit Mal. bowing himself backwards.*
Card. And where wilt *thou* be?   Hop'st thou to go free,
Charg'd with that perilous secret?   Could I bind
Thy lips forever, think'st thou I could brook
Thy insolent mien, where even now I read,
As in thy cover'd taunts and ill-tim'd jests,
Abhorrently familiar! swollen presumption,
Bred of a conscious partnership in crime —
Could I bear this? from thee?   Or would I trust
The servant who his loving lord betray'd
To ruin and death?   No, thou vile tool!   To-day
Complete thy function, which the will of fate
Proffers to my ambition and revenge:
To-morrow —   I will break thy edge forever!
                    [*Exit into the same
                cabinet as before (in Scene III.)*

SCENE VI.

An Antechamber leading to the G. Duchess's
Apartments in the Pitti.

SIGNORA MALOCUORE,
passing slowly and thoughtfully through.   She stops
suddenly midway.

Sign. [40] [*to herself.*] Donna Virginia! I were better pleas'd
To want her sweet simplicity.

Enter
from the door facing her, and which is supposed
to lead to the G. Duchess's Apartments,
DONNA VIRGINIA.

Aloud.] Is 't so?
Donna Virginia absent from the chase?
How shall her friend and royal sister spare her?
Virg. Better than would I hope my loyal lord,
Who stays behind, being slightly indispos'd.
But what keeps you, Signora, from Caiano?
Sign. A like and yet a different cause.   My lord,
Though loyal I hope, will better do without me;
And I am ailing too.

Virg. That is a jest.

Sign. Then seriously." I like Caiano much;
   The Villa Poggio more. The distance, scarce
   An hour's easy drive, is soon gone through.
   And passing-well I love the autumnal chase,
   When the wind rustling through the scant-leav'd forest
   Calls blood into the faded cheek, and dote
   On royal banquets, where the cost and care
   Are not my portion, but the pleasure is.
   But, as it happen'd, my well-loving spouse
   Seem'd in no very loving mood to-day:
   And so, to avoid the infliction of his spleen,
   I supervise the change the Duchess order'd
   In the blue hangings of the Silver'd Chamber
   (Whence now I think your Highness comes,) more
         pleas'd
   To glad one person than to worry two.

Virg. Happily said; and, surely, kindly done.
   Now could I envy you the sweet bright smile
   That will reward your forethought.

                        Sign. O for that,
   So chary has the Duchess been to me
   Of smiles and sweetness, I have long forgotten
   There was such blessing: and this time, methinks,
   She will have no will to grant it.

                        Virg. Ah, you point
   To her strange sadness. Just before she left,
   I ask'd what ail'd her. Kissing me, she answer'd,
   "Nothing in health"; then, with a pensive smile,

As though it irk'd her to seem so deject,
Added, "There is a weight upon my heart;
A sad foreboding : it will all have gone,
Ere next we meet." So saying, she embrac'd me,
Then, parting, gaz'd a moment in my face
Wistful and sad, and press'd my hand. Her eyes —
Were wet with tears.

     Sign. As yours are now, Madonna.
This is illusion.   The dejected spirits,
Pressing upon the heart, allow these phantoms
To cloud the unwary brain."   Who has not seen,
In sickness, or when brooding care makes sleep
Desert the wearying pillow, monstrous forms,
Or bodiless heads, misshapen, that still come
Nearer and nearer, spreading on the eye
More large and hideous, and in sequence close,
Rank upon rank, in tapering vista long ;
The last dim phantom lessening to a point,
Lost in the far perspective ? Of such stuff
Were fashion'd these sick bodements. It is said,
The Cardinal and our royal Lady quarrel'd.
This haply has depress'd her lively spirit,
And made your parting mournful.   Did your Grace
Remark their greeting ere the train took horse ?
Virg. I thought the Duchess' mien constrain'd and cold.
 Yet was it courteous : and the Duke's demeanor,
Gracious and kind as wonted, veil'd it all.
I think none else would note it, but who knew
There had been words between them.

Sign. And himself?

Virg. There was — perhaps I fancied it — at times
A strange abstraction in the Cardinal's looks,
Which, fix'd on vacancy, appear'd to see
Or seek for something.   Once, when in this mood,
The Duke address'd him.   Visibly he started,
And — so I thought — turn'd deadly pale.   But then
He came from his apartment looking pale.

Sign. Doubtless 't was fancy — as your Highness knew
A cause for discomposure.
                              Virg. But 't was not
Fancy, I saw him eye the Duchess once
With mortal hatred.   May I be forgiven
If I misjudge my father's blood, or wrong
A Christian prelate!   but the look was one
That made my heart stand still.
                              Sign. It cannot be.
The Cardinal-Prince reveres — that know I well!
Or, rather, loves his royal brother's spouse,
As truly as — myself, who from the first
Was wedded to her fortunes, — nay, with love
And reverence equal to my honest lord's,
Whose rare devotion none can doubt.
                              Virg. Indeed!
Heaven grant it be so!   Heaven itself must grieve
Over these unnatural discords.   Yet I doubt.
The Duchess' heart has had some heavy shock. —
But I must not detain you, dear Signora;
And my lord looks for me. [*going.*

Sign. [*attending her.*] Ah, happy lord !
And happier lady ! When you have been wed,
As I have been, for two and twenty years,
Your Prince will be more patient, and yourself,
Believe me, much less anxious.

                Virg. Fie, Signora!
Why, when our hearts are happy in their Spring,
Warn us that Autumn 's coming? But I know
The sere and yellow leaf is not for us,
Whose souls shall know no season in their loves,
Like Francis and Bianca's.

              Sign. O'er whose soul
Come shadows of the Winter even now.

        Exit VIRGINIA *attended by*
    the SIGNORA, — *who presently re-enters.*

Like *them ?* Thou simple one! What, should I say
"Heaven grant it be so"! Little couldst thou think
That wish would threaten —— Is it death to both?
I fear me Malocnor has gone too far.
He hates the proud Venetian; the deep wounds
Inflicted by her scorn more sorely rankle
In his dark brooding spirit than mine; the slight
Put on him, when the dead Intendant's friend,
Sennuccio, rose to favor, has given perhaps
Desperate impulsion to the bold designs
Wherein the Cardinal-Prince has long involv'd him.
This childish-hearted lady took no note

Of what I saw, and trembled as I saw,
When Malocuor, by order of the Duke,
Spurr'd on before the cavalcade, to see
That everything was ready. Even now
Perhaps the deed is doing! Help us God!
I would prevent it if I could: but what,
What know I? what dare hint, whose very thought
Is but conjecture? Oh, that heavy thought!
Would, would 't were morrow, and the Duke were
   safe!

       Exit, by the door whence VIRGINIA
         had entered.

SCENE VII.

A rich Hall in the magnificent Villa del Poggio.
At the top of the scene, a large folding-door, partially open,
gives a view of the Banqueting-Room, brilliantly
illuminated. The tables set out, etc., etc.

There is an uproar — the guests are risen
from their seats, in various attitudes of consternation
and horror. The GRAND DUKE *and* DUCHESS *are seen*
supported in the arms of SENNUCCIO *and others, while*
before them stands the CARDINAL, *gesticu-*
lating and ordering.

Enter
from the Banqueting-Room, through
the open doors, and in precipitation, the
DUKE OF BRACCIANO, *followed as hurriedly by* ABBIOSO, —
both with looks of dismay and horror ; and, less
impetuously, from the side scene, with hat on
and mantle, and spurred, DON PIETRO.

Don P. What is this noise, Orsini ? Thou art pale
And horror-stricken !
               Bracc. 'T is the end of things.
The Duke and Duchess are both poison'd.
                              Don P. Poison'd !
How ? and by whom ?
               Bracc. Think whom their death would profit;
Then say by whom ? Let Abbioso speak.

DON PIETRO *stands as if stupefied, looking on them both,*
then, while ABBIOSO *speaks, gazing on the scene*
in the Banqueting-Room.

Abb. [*speaking hurriedly.*
The Duchess press'd the Cardinal to partake

Of a white sweetmeat, which he still refus'd
On plea of health derang'd. The Duke and she,
Eagerly eating, suddenly were seiz'd
With mortal pangs. The cry arose, of Poison!
The Cardinal, pointing to a ring he wore,
Declar'd the stone, through Providence, had warn'd
     him,
And charg'd the Duchess loudly with the crime.

Don P. With what design? How could it profit *her?*
'T is well for me I sit not next the throne:
He might have laid this devil's-work to me.

Bracc. He has sent to seize the fortresses already.
The troops are order'd out. All in his name.

Don P. These were his speculations for my good!

*Facing once more the Banqueting-Room, he moves a step as
     if to go to it, then stops, and, adjusting his mantle:*

I 'll not look on this scene. I cannot aid them.
And righteous Cain must face his God alone.

Bracc. We both were fleeing. Isabella's death
Might lend the new Duke pretext for his hate
Against the Orsini.

              Abb. And my stubborn tongue
Has not sung anthems in his Highness' praise.

Don P. I will ride back.

*Through the doors of the Banqueting-Room,
attendants are seen carrying out the* GRAND DUKE
and BIANCA, *the* CARDINAL *following. The guests dispersing
or gazing on each other in mute horror.*

Don Pietro *throws a hurri.d look on the scene,*
and is about to leave hastily by the side where he had entered, —
Bracciano *and* Abbioso, *in like manner, at the*
opposite side, — when, Enter through the
folding-door, Archbishop of Pisa,
Bentivoglio, *and others.*

What now? What means that movement?

Archb. His Grace has order'd that the dying pair
Be carried to the Vaulted Room.

Don. P. The sole
Disfurnish'd and dark chamber in the house!

Denti. And suffers none to follow.

Abb. God in Heaven!

Bracc. 'T is time we fled.

Don P. Till better days, Farewell.
Exeunt, hurriedly,
Don Pietro *at one side,* Bracciano *and* Abbioso *at the other.*

The Archbishop *and the rest, who*
group around him, remain; and other guests, both lords
and ladies, are seen coming from the Ban-
queting-Room, as the scene, closing,
gives place to

SCENE VIII. AND LAST.

*A gloomy, vaulted chamber, with a single arched doorway.
There is no furniture but a large armed-chair. And
the room is almost totally dark.*

*Enter
through the arch
the* CARDINAL; *the* GRAND DUKE
and BIANCA, *supported in the arms of servants;*
SENNUCCIO, *bearing up* BIANCA's *head. Then*
MALOCUORE, *holding a lighted torch.*

Card. Set them down here.

BIANCA *is placed tenderly in the great chair
by* SENNUCCIO. *The* GRAND DUKE *rests on the floor at her
feet, his head upon her knees.*

Retire ye.   [*Exeunt servants.*
To Mal.] Let none in.
G. D. A fire is in my entrails. O my God!
Is there no help? Have pity, Ferdinand, brother!
Senn. I have sent for both your surgeons, dear my lord.
One must now soon be here.

Card. [*in a voice of thunder.*

Who bade thee, dog?

Make fast the door. [*to Mal.*

MALOCOURE *putting his torch through a socket*
projecting from the wall of the chamber,
bolts the door.

They shall not enter here
Till Heaven's act of vengeance is gone through.

Senn. [*leaving the G. Duke.*

I will go forth, oppose who may or dare,
And make this treason public. Thou, [*drawing on Mal.*
stand back!

Card. Guard the door, Malocuore! If he strive,
Stab thou the gray-hair'd traitor to the heart!

SENNUCCIO *and* MALOCUORE — *the latter his back against*
• *the door — cross swords.*

G. D. Forbear, Sennuccio! On thy oath! Sole friend,
Thou canst not stead us: aid would come too late.
O Ferdinand! could not *my* life suffice?
Must thy fangs rend this innocent victim too?

Bian. [*who has hitherto hung over her lord,*
lifting now her head.

Die with the spirit of a man, my lord.
Appeal not to that tiger.

Card. Hast thou found
Thy speech at last, vile sorceress? It was thou,
Thou with thy black enchantments and damn'd drugs.

Hast done this deed.   The dose was meant for **me**.
But thy weak husband took it unforewarn'd;
And thou, to escape the punishment ——

     Bian. Of what?

Knows not the world, that poisoning my lord,
Of will or not, I had done thee precious service?
Thou seek'st to make me guilty, yet thou knowest
I bear within me what might blast thy hopes,
Could I but live so long to give it life.
For this, and thy defeated criminal passion ——

G. D. Water! water! for the love of God!
  Is there no drop?

    Bian. And thou seest this, unmov'd!   ∘
            [*to Card.*

And thou, O God, art witness unto all!

G. D. I die, Bianca.   Let thy — arms — thy lips ——
  With an effort, he raises himself on one knee.
   Embracing, she kisses, him.   He falls,
    dead, across her feet.

Bian. My lord!   My lord! ——
      I will not wail thee long. —
Sennuccio, hear. —   O agony! this thirst! —
Give — give me breath awhile, kind Heaven! —
         Sennuccio, —
The laws of God, thou seest, are irreversible, —
And even our indiscretions — soon or late —
Come to the judgment, and are all amerc'd.

Tell — tell my sire, this punishment I bear —
In just requital — of my disregard
Of his parental anguish, my neglect
Of my first duty — when — I fled my home ;
And pray him — that he will not — not remember
His child unkindly — for the one great sin —
Of all her life. [*Dies.*

SENNUCCIO, *who has knelt on one knee reverently
before her, kissing her hand, takes now this hand in both of
his, and bends his head over it — remaining in
this attitude to the end.*

Mal. [*taking his torch from the socket and holding it
over Bianca.*
          'T is finish'd. [*Inverts the torch, against the
                    floor, and extinguishes it.*
     Card. [*coldly.*] It is well.
Throw back the door, and let the crowd swarm in.

MALOCUORE *opens wide the door, and a strong
light from within, as from an illuminated corridor,
is poured upon the group, — while
Enter,* ARCHBISHOP OF PISA, BENTIVOGLIO,
and others of the Court.

Behold the consummation of the crime!

Let the Great Duke have burial meet his rank:
The sorceress fling into the public vaults.

[*Exit, followed by Malocuor.*

*The spectators gather solemnly round
the partially lighted bodies* — SENNUCCIO *still keeping
his position* — BIANCA *lying back in the
chair, the* GRAND DUKE *across her
feet* — *and slowly the*

Curtain falls.

NOTES

NOTES TO BIANCA CAPELLO

1.—P. 206. *A shout, Pietro* —] The remark made in Note (and sub-note) 2, of "The Double Deceit," (vol. IV. p. 255,) applies in this instance. The name, like *Bianca*, is made a trisyllable. But, though it is so far anglicized (with others in the play), let the Actor sound *i* as *e* and *e* as *a*. So with the fictitious and character-name *Sennuccio**: although, by separating the two final vowels, it is made to be of four syllables, give it otherwise the Italian pronunciation, and sound it *Sen-noot'-che-o*.

Bracciano, too, (*Act* III., *Sc.* 3,) though it is less important, has the first *c* sounded as *t*. In Italian, it is but of three syllables (*Brat-chah'-no*); in the text, it is of four.

2.—P. 210. *Then softly bade me rise and speak.*] For the Stage, omit from here to "My thoughts came back," nine lines below.

3.—P. 213. *Desires he feels not. Affluence clips the wings. Of honesty which flies distress*—] For the Stage, substitute, as more directly intelligible:

---

* *Sennino;* diminutive of *Senno:* applied jocosely, but without disparagement, to a person who, while yet young, has the gravity, the serious manners, and the prudence of age. We have a corresponding phrase, but comic and somewhat vulgar, and partaking of the grotesque, in the compound *Sobersides.*

" Emotions that he feels not. Wealth binds down [secures]
The honesty that yields to want."

Or :

" Emotions that he feels not. Wealth keeps home
The honesty that flies distress "—

4.—P. 231. —*board.*] For the Stage, read " pallet."

5.—P. 236. *Forget thy art.*] More plainly, for the Stage : " Deal
frankly once." Or, read the verse :

" Forget the courtier. What is said of late ? "

6.—P. 242. *Who has,* etc.] Or, if the Actress prefer it,
" O hate me not! who have one only grief,
The thought that thou art pining unconsol'd "——

7.—P. 253. *Her natural pride* —] See Note 22.

8.—P. 256. *Francis has cloister'd her*—] This he did on the very
day of Cosmo's decease, who had most liberally dowered Camilla.
With this exception, says Galluzzi, Francesco acted conscientiously
in all his father's trusts and legacies. *Istor. del Granduc. di Toscana
sotto il Gov. della Casa Medici* (Firenze 1781, in 4to), t. ii. pp. 239, 240.
Previously, (p. 176,) he tells us, she attempted to dominate the whole
Court, to be the dispenser of favors, and sowed discord between
father and son. And (p. 179): the Cardinal Ferdinand curried favor
with Camilla, and obtained through her considerable sums of money
for his lavish expenditures in Rome.—Whatever therefore the policy
of the measure, the new Grand-duke may have felt himself justified
in putting this dangerous woman under restraint ; and subsequently,
when, as will be seen, he released her on the marriage of her daughter
Donna Virginia, her house became the rendezvous of the conspirators
who, with the secret impulsion and aid of the Cardinal, rendered
Francesco's reign and life at all times more or less unquiet.

9.—P. 257. — *whose near death   Must come of Victor's triumph !*] This, as the exclamation-point denotes, is said ironically by *Malocuor*, who appears to be reciting after what he calls the "psalms." But the historian just quoted, with his prejudice against Bianca, and his steadfast purpose (unknown perhaps to himself, yet obvious enough to his readers) to leave nothing unused that can be presented against her, or against the Grand-duke, whom he seems to hold in equal dislike, gravely recounts as a fact (ii. 299) what I have here made to be predicted as a malignant and extravagant calculation of the event. See *Append. II.* y. 1578.

10.—P. 257. The two princesses Exeunt, *etc.*] The profligate Isabella is described as highly accomplished. It is credible. The Medici were not wanting in talent, whatever their moral deficiencies. To beauty and grace, says the historian of that House, she added letters, poetry, music, and the practice of various languages. *Granducato ;* ii. 268. It is noticeable that he touches very lightly, scarcely indeed perceptibly, the licentiousness of this princess.— See, in Appendix II., p. 378.

11.—P. 259. *But screen'd his strumpet sister in my spite.*] This line is characteristic. But, if preferred for the Stage, it may read :

> " But kept my missives back, to screen his sister."

12.—P. 276. *Master Cappelli* —] "Ciascuno si chiama a Firenze per . . . *ec.*, e s' usa comunemente, se non v' è distinzione di grado e di molta età, dire tu e non voi a un solo, e solo a' cavalieri a' dottori ed a canonici si dà del messere, come a medici del *maestro*, ed a frati del padre." VARCHI. *Storia Fior.* III. p. 118, ed. Mil. (8°. 1803.)

13.—P. 279. The Drop falls.] Here the play, being so far complete in itself, may, for the purposes of representation, be made occasionally to terminate, giving thus a shorter drama, although not finishing the tragedy as it is told in history.

Further, though there is a considerable interval of time between all the Acts, the license of the romantic drama being in that respect stretched to the utmost, and though the space of time between the 4th and 5th Acts is greater than that between the 3d and 4th, yet it strikes me as worthy of suggestion, that when the whole of the play is represented it might be well to have some interlude, of music or otherwise, between the falling of the Drop on the death of *Bonaventuri* and the rising of it again on the announcement of *Bianca* as Grand-duchess. Such leaps for the imagination of the spectator are, it is true, no more considered in our English drama, than they are for the reader, who makes them easily everywhere; but it might be an aid to the illusion nevertheless, to adopt the hint I have suggested.

14.—P. 280. —*Have her witch's-arts Enchanted too your Highness?*] See latter half of Note 22, and in Appendix II. the 4th paragraph under y. 1576.

15.—P. 281. SCENE II.] Or, the first Scene continued, if preferred, with simply the new Entry: "*Enter from opposite sides,* etc."

16.—P. 283. *Met at Firenzuöl the pompous train.*] Or, for the Stage,
                              Rode forth to meet the ninety in advance:
namely, the ninety Venetian nobles, mentioned in Act IV., Sc. 4, (page 294.) *Firenzuola* is five miles from Florence (*Firenze.*)

The description of the pomp of the Venetian embassy and of its reception, of the solemn espousals of the Grand-duke with Bianca and her coronation as Queen of Cyprus, as given in Scenes 4 and 5 of Act IV., is historical.

17.—P. 285. *Our beast still ramp'd where gleams the lilied crown.*] That is, from the *crest*. This gave way to the *crown*, granted, as the pretentious legend on its circle indicates, by Pope Pius V. to Cosmo. To mollify the people, the centre of the circle bore a large red *lily*, the emblem of the Republic.

Roundle is the general name for a circular *charge*. But in the arms of Medici, the tincture of the roundles being *gules* (red), and their shape convex (like a bun or a button), their specific name is *torteaux* or *torteauxes.* In Italian however these charges are called *palle* (balls)*, which name comes nearer to the *pellets* ("gun-stones") of English heraldry ; but the *pellet* is tinctured *sable.* The reigning branch of the Medici carried *or six torteaux* ("sei palle rosse in campo d' oro")—six red balls in a field of gold. Of the three which are *in chief* (upper third of the shield) the central one after 1465 was blazoned, by concession of the King of France, "in segno di singulare affezione," (Vinc. Borgh. *ut infra cit.*) with three *fleurs-de-lys* of gold, and therefore it was made *azure.* . ·

For the verse in the text may be redd by the Stage : "Our gonfalon bore not the ducal crown."

18.—P. 285. *God's might ! the throne of Clement's bastard son, etc.*]
That is of the first Duke (or *Doge*, as was his title of installation,) Alessandro, who, although accounted a natural son of Lorenzo the Younger (Duke of Urbino) by a simple country-girl,† was more than

---

* It is easy to see that this species of charge in the escutcheon would subject the Medici to the malice of their defamers, who said it represented the *pills* of the ancestral profession. This saying at least had humor in it ; but the explanation of their flatterers, who would have it be emblematic of the marks made by the mace of a giant named *Mugello* killed by Averardo under Charlemagne (See Litta: *Fam. Cel. Ital.* (Milano 1825, in fol.) vol. ii.) is simply absurd. In fact these balls are of frequent occurrence in the arms of other Florentine families, as of the *Foraboschi,* the *Cipriani,* the *Squarcialupi,* etc. V. Borghini: *Dell' Arme delle Famigl. Fior.* (Fiorenz. 1585. in 4to, P. ii p. 57.) Some of the Medici bore seven *palle,* some eight. (*ib.* p. 78.) I think it not unlikely that the design arose from the bosses or studs which are sometimes seen in ancient bucklers. In the escutcheon of 1373, the peculiar crest from which issues the demi beast, whatever that be, rampant, is strewed with them,—in heraldic phrase, *semé of torteaux.*

† When the Florentine exiles, or their partisans, wrote upon the walls of his lodging at Rome, in allusion to his mother's place of birth, " Viva Alessandro da Collevecchio," he merely laughed, saying, he *was obliged to them for having*

suspected of being a bastard of Pope Clement VII.'s.* (See VARCHI. IV., p. 344.) The mother herself was uncertain which of the two had the better claim to him.—*Granduc.* Introd. xxxii. *V.* App. I. n. 9. c

Cosmo (or *Cosimo*, as the Italians write it), the successor of Alessandro (who left no legitimate children) and the father of Francesco and Don Pietro, was of a collateral branch of the Medici, being fourth in descent from the younger brother of the first Cosmo. Hence the epithet, " unlineal."

As to the origin of this renowned family, Sansovino (*Della Origine e de' Fatti delle Famigl. Illus. d' Italia ;* 4to., 1582 : a mere catalogue) recounts (citing Villani) the absurd fiction which made their descent from rulers in Greece. Galluzzi (*Istor,* ec. supra cit.) says their enemies reproached them with many low conditions : " di aver fatto il Carbonaio in Mugello†, l' Oste e il Biscazziere [*professional gambler*]

taught him whence he was, which he did not know before.—VARCHI. *Stor.,* ec., V. 193. Galluzzi says she was a housemaid.—*Introd.* p. xxxii.

* Clement VII. (Giulio de' Medici), himself illegitimate, had two illegitimate nephews, one the Alessandro above, the other Ippolito son of Giuliano. It was left to his option by the Emperor Charles V, which of the two should be made the head of their House and prince of the Republic. Ippolito is described by Varchi as adorned with every grace of mind and body : " Era Ippolito Cardinal de' Medici in sul più bel fiore dell' età, non avendo più di ventun' anno," [his competitor was a year younger]; " era bellissimo e grato d' aspetto, era di felicissimo ingegno, era pieno di tutte le grazie e virtù, era affabile e alla mano con ognuno, era come quegli che ritraeva alla magnificenza e benignità di Leone, e non alla scarsità e parsimonia di Clemente, liberalissimo verso tutti gli uomini eccellenti, o in arme o in lettere, o in qualsivoglia altra dell' arti liberali, ec." (*Stor.* iv. 345 sq.) Yet that true Pontiff, the slave of passion and of predilection and prejudice, and guided in public policy by a love of power without scrupulousness and by the dictates of a supposed self-interest that rendered him incapable of the wisdom of a statesman, preferred to this princely character the profligate and incompetent Alexander. And this choice confirmed the belief of his paternity.

† Fifteen miles from Florence.— There was the villa of Cosmo, the second *Duke*, at the time of his election.

in Firenze, e di avere avuto un Medico, ec." Their adulators derived
them from Consuls and Emperors of Rome. Their reasonable origin
is from a physician, said (by those who hold a middle course) to
have been of Charlemagne. Galluzzi dates however the known rise of
the Medici from Averardo (son of Averardo *who was Podestà* [Chief
Magistrate, Bailiff (in the old sense) or Mayor] of Lucca, 1230), who
accumulated by commerce great riches,* divided in 1319 between his
six sons. (*Ist.* I. pp. x, xi.) In the genealogical chart prefixed to
Varchi's History, Averardo (surnamed *Bicci* or *Di Bicc*) is the base,
and from him Giovanni rising is made *Gonfaloniere*, (literally, standard-
bearer, as the moderns say *Alfiere*, but used like *Podestà*, to indicate the
Chief Magistrate of the city,)† in 1421. The actual reign of the Medici
as *Dukes* of Florence (through the subversion of the liberty of their
country by Papal intrigues and the power of Austria) dates only from
Alessandro just mentioned, the seventh in descent from Averardo,
in the year 1532.

For Bianca's blood, Galluzzi says (ii. 84) : " Her father, besides the
great authority which he had in the Republic, was connected by rela-
tionship with its principal families. He had for his second wife a
daughter of the House of Grimani, sister of the Patriarch of Aquileia."

19.—P. 286. —*the Pregadi.*] The Venetian Senate.

20. —P. 287. *Let her, I say, Beware the Cardinal Medici's crooked
fang.*] The entire *Scene* expresses my deliberate opinion as to the

---

* We see thus easily how, as Varchi observes (I. 3), partly by their prudence
and liberality, partly through the imprudence and avarice of others, but not
without long trials and contests, among which must be counted their banishment
from Florence three times in ninety-four years, the House of Medici attained
in fact, but not as yet in name, and in the face of perpetual enmities, and with
the drawback of undying and dangerous hatred, the mastery of the Republic. ·

† " E nel vero la signoria col gonfaloniere, e massimamente senza l' appello, era
magistrato tirannico, e *per mezzo di lei*, oltra mille altri scandoli e sollevamenti,
si fece Cosimo poco meno che padrone assoluto di Firenze " VARCHI. IV. 342.

history of the Grand-duchess Bianca. Taken with Appendix I., it will
supersede with those who care not for authorities, and scarcely trouble
themselves at all with notes in a work of this nature, any exposition
derived from the carelessness, the want of insight into character, or
the criminal misrepresentation of historians. The more studious
reader will find every satisfaction in Appendix II. — The *Biographie
Universelle* indicates a Life of *Bianca* in these words : " Siebenkees a
écrit une vie de B. C. d' après les sources originales, Gotha 1739, in
8° . . . traduite en anglais par Ludger." This translation is on the
Catalogue of the N. Y. Society Library, but has disappeared in some
manner from its shelves, for after repeated inquiries I have failed to
obtain any knowledge of its existence.

21.—P. 283. *The sorrow that*, etc.] For the Stage, omit these two
verses.   ‘

22.—P. 289. *Titian, had he liv'd,   Had pointed to the air of native
pride   That dignifies thy beauty, and had said*, etc.] Noble saw two
likenesses of her at Strawberry Hill, one a miniature, the other a portrait ; " the former [taken] when Bianca was at the height of her
charms, the other not long before her death. * * * Her countenance,"
he adds, " discovers that native pride which made her scorn to be
anything less than wife even to a sovereign." *Mem. Illus. House of
Medici** (Lond. 8°. 1797,) p. 287 *sq.* Although his argument, that, if she
had yielded before marriage, the Duke " would have been content
with her favors without marrying her," (p. 278,) I do not consider
tenable,† yet the quality of mind he ascribes to our heroine, if he did

---

* An inaccurate and superficial work, which, although I have made use of it for
the purposes of the drama, I cite only for the interesting item of the pictures.

† And in fact there is the example of Cosmo, who married Camilla Martelli after
she had borne him Donna Virginia. A better confirmation of our heroine's chastity would be found perhaps in the fact of her private marriage with the Grand-
duke. This ceremony was performed by the Duke's confessor two months after
the death of Joanna (1578), according to Galluzzi, who adds: *the guardianship*

not mistake the pictured expression, is such as does not accord with low profligacy, much less with the despicable traits which Galluzzi imputes to her, who indeed thereby contradicts his own description. "Assai potenti," he has said, speaking of Bianca when Francesco was yet but Prince, "erano le attrative di questa giovine, poichè oltre i meriti della bellezza aveva ancora ottenuto dalla natura un ingegno tale che somministrava tutte le arti per rendersi l' arbitra del suo amante. *Le grazie, la vivacità congiunta con una certa facondia*," ec. (pp. 87, 88, t. e.) This fascination the public were taught to consider the result of magic arts and of philters ; and the eulogist of the Cardinal Grand-duke has not hesitated gravely to record the scandal. See in *Appendix II.* "y. 1576," 4th paragraph.

Titian, who (as said in *Act I. Sc. 4.*,) actually painted Bianca, (See Append. III.) died three years before the point of time in the text.

23.—P. 290. *Joy for the offspring, hope of which I nurse—*] From this line to the close of the passage, the Stage will substitute :

> For my throne's heritage, thou this day shalt be
> Dower'd by thy country with those honors which
> The world will value. Thy true crown is here.

24.—P. 290. *When Your Highness' brother—*] Omit from here to " But for this cause,"— seventh line below.

of the three princesses took away suspicion from her living in the Palace. Had Bianca yielded her favors already, there had been no need of a private marriage, and if her amour with the Duke were notorious, there could have been, in the first place, no occasion for avoiding suspicion, and secondly, if attempted by such an artifice it would not have been successful. Not to say, that a known mistress of the Grand-duke would not have been appointed guardian to his female children, although, as in the case of Mad. de Genlis, a *liaison* simply suspected would offer no impediment. But all argument falls to the ground if it be fact that Don Antonio de' Medici, whether really her son or only imposed upon the Grand-duke as such (as Galluzzi would have it), was publicly recognized as illegitimate. See *Appendix II.* y. 1576 ; also *ib.* note 24, p. 403.

25.—P. 291. *Twice happy*, etc.] Omit here five lines.

26.—P. 298. The Ambassadors —] Omit from here to "About this hour," (ninth line below.)

27.—P. 299. *My father*, etc.] Omit to " But I should shame to own."

28.—P. 299. *And her too* —] Omit to "This coronation over,"— seven verses.

29.—P. 299. *She cannot live*, etc.] The most difficult point for me to get over in the biased statements of the hostile historians is Bianca's expressions to the Cardinal at the close of the y. 1580 (in a letter): "Io vivo più a lei che a me, poichè vivo in lei, per il che senza lei non posso vivere, *ee.*"—(*Granduc.* ii. 344.) See, besides the *Cardinal's* own doubts in the succeeding lines, what turn *Bianca* is made to give to them in *Act* V. *Sc.* I. They are however too extravagant, I will not say to be genuine, (for I have known at least one spiritual and vivacious woman of high breeding and of proud temper, and who possessed that very fluency of language which Galluzzi ascribes to Bianca, to indulge in quite as extravagant terms of affection in writing to a stranger to her blood, neither husband nor lover, and with even less motive)*—but too extravagant to seem genuine ; and the malice that did not hesitate to blacken her in other respects would find no compunction against such a counterfeit. But supposing them to be truly of Bianca's writing, and that they are not to be interpreted by any vivacity of disposition and vanity of eloquence, what follows ? That there was more than a legitimate attachment between the Cardinal and his brother's wife. And this is to concede the whole point in discussion, and to justify, even historically, the part I have, equally with the romancer (or romancers,) assigned to the Cardinal. V. Append. I.

---

* One thing is worth observing : such persons cannot be sincere. If Bianca did write that letter, she was wanting in candor.

30.—P. 300. *No, it were better*, etc.] Omit to "As yet,"—eleventh line below ; then omit the words " To rectify this wrong."

31.—P. 309. *From taint by such a traitor — traitor, ay !*] Which may read, at the option of the Theatre :

> From taint by such a traitor.
>
> *Card.* Traitor!
>
> *Bian.* Ay!

32.—P. 310. *Death ! 'I should sink to this !*] Or, avoiding the ellipsis : "Death ! Am I come to this !"

33.—P. 320. *She might have had*, etc.] This was his mistress, a handsome woman, whom he had brought back with him from Madrid in 1584. The Prince in his profligacy seemed to expect that she would be admitted at Court, and was displeased when Bianca, as was natural and proper, refused to receive her. V. *Granduc.* II. 387.

34.—P. 322. *The Pope gives dispensation —*] See *Appendix II.* at y. 1585.

Immediately before the verse (in *Act* III. *Sc.* 4.),

> " When I throw off this purple which I hate,"

occurred in the first MS. the following three verses. They were superfluous, therefore weak. I introduce them here simply to illustrate the text above, and, historically, the Cardinal's ambitious and intriguing character, which was in fact the character of a true churchman where ambitious,—profligately so.

> The Pope is my creation, hence my creature.
>
> For he sees not, weak man, that not of love,
>
> But for my ends, I help'd to heave him up.

35.—P. 326. *Wrought by the Duchess and a Jewish hag   Confederate in her sorceries*, etc.] See Appendix II., y. 1576.

36.—P. 328. Waiter brings wine and glasses, is paid and retires.]

But to keep up the life and variety of the picture in the background, he moves about in the discharge of his functions, carrying flasks etc. *to the different tables.* — The Stage requires hints of this kind, but I am sorry to think is not likely to observe them.

37.—P. 331. *Not Cini's surgery* —] Cini was the Cardinal's physician.

38.—P. 332. *Whose lightning, hurtled by the lion's cub*, etc.] Or, for the Stage :

> Whose lightning, hurl'd by Peter Leoncll,
>
> Whom men call Cardinal Farnese's son,
>
> Frightens the confines with its devious blaze.

"Lion's cub" is an allusion to the name *Lioncillo* (leoncello.)

This miscreant was actually at the head of the large number of men named in the text. The historian tells us, that brigandage and assassination had come to be considered knightly service. As now-a-days in Italy the Church has been, from political motives or from indifference to the public welfare, the great supporter of such wretches, so in those times it was the Church-feudatories chiefly that had them in service. See *Append.* II. y. 1580, ¶ 2, —also y. 1575, ¶ 2. As men above the vulgar herd joined these blood-bands, the language at least attributed to the assassins in the text is not greatly beyond their degree, whatever may be thought of their sentiments.

39.—P. 332. *They put wise Machiavelli to the rack* —] This was nearly a century before. Machiavelli died in 1527, sixty years before the time of the Scene. But the condition of things was not much changed from that of his troubled day, and his was a name not easily to be forgotten, any more than that of "Antichrist" (Clement VII.)

40.- P. 337. Sign.] For the Stage, commence: "Donna Virginia absent *etc.?*"

41.—P. 338. *Then seriously.*] Omit to "my well-loving spouse," and read the passage :

Then seriously, thus. My loving spouse
Seem'd *etc.*

After which, make the last two lines of the part:

In the blue hangings of the Silver'd Room, more pleas'd
To glad *etc.*

43.—P. 339. *Who has not seen* —] Omit to " It is said," ninth line
below, reading the verse :

To cloud the unwary brain. 'Tis freely said.

Then omit, from "Did your Grace," thirty-one lines, reading thus,
from the commencement of the alteration :

And made your parting mournful.

Virg. Yet I doubt
The Duchess' heart *etc.*

Or in fine, omit, in the performance, the entire Scene, which was
written merely to interpose time between the revelation of Malacuor's
design and its perpetration. But our English Stage (as I have elsewhere had occasion to remark) sets time and space at defiance ; and
the accustomed audience rarely protests against any violation of
probability that saves them from fatigue.

ADDITION TO NOTE 18.

The influence of a family of wealth will depend greatly upon its numbers and
its ramifications. Galluzzi, as an evidence of the potency of the Medici, records this
fact, that even after the pestilence of 1348, there were no less than fifty males of
that House surviving. *Introd.* xi. Without this numerical preponderance, it
may be questioned whether, notwithstanding their riches and their talents, their
ambition could have made head against the determined opposition of their rivals
and of the better lovers of their country.

Of the Capelli, Bern. Segni, who wrote under Francesco, particularizes the ambassador Carlo, mentioned in the text (*Act.* 1. *Sc.* IV.), who, he tells us, raised in
Florence a monument to his horse, which was standing in his, the historian's day.
Storie Fior. vol. i. *ed.* Milan, (1805, in 8°) p. 225. We may suppose the Cardinal Grand-duke, in his anxiety to remove every object that might recall the
memory of Bianca (*Append.* II. prope fin.), ordered this monument, whatever it
was, to be destroyed. Another Capello (Vincent) is mentioned by the same historian as being General of the Venetians. *Ib.* ii. 151.

APPENDICES

I.

The following observations, intended at the time as the sole appendix to the play, were written six years after the completion of the latter, when I had forgotten that I had so fully illustrated in my text every particular that bears upon the story, as to render any comment or explanation needless. Still, as a brief analysis of the historic question involved, they may not be uninteresting to the general reader.

The footnotes are of the date of the transcription.

For many of the incidents, and even for the groundwork or suggestive type of some of the characters in *Bianca Capello*, I am largely indebted to the romance of the same name by A. G. Meissner (*Leipz.* in 16to, 1784), who probably obtained his particulars from the collection of Celio Malespini of Verona, *Part.* II. *Nov.* 84, which I have not seen, but find particularized by Galluzzi as conspicuous among several written on Bianca's fortunes.(1)

---

(1) *Granducato*, ii. p. 85. The historian speaks of *Mondragone* and his wife as intermediary, in the romance, between the Grand-duke and Bianca, but, with his usual inconsiderate or malevolent bias, only to cast a slur upon the latter by remarking that the Duke had found no need of go-betweens. Francesco might have, and, with still more likelihood, would have found the need, in his position, even were Bianca the "vile seducer" that Galluzzi and his copyists make her.

The character of Bianca will always perhaps be a subject of historical doubt. The weight of authority is against her. She was probably weaker than I have made her (2); but I do not believe she was depraved or grossly criminal. The historian of the Grand-duchy of Tuscany has spared no pains to render her atrocious. His large work,

But that is not the point. *Mondragone* is introduced by that very name, and with his wife, in that very function, by Meissner. He is the *Malocuore* of the Tragedy.

In Roscoe's *Italian Novelists*, vol. III. (Lond. in 8°. 1886), some specimens are given of Celio, but not the story of Bianca. Celio Malespini, who held, we are told, the post of Secretary to Francesco, is supposed to have begun writing his numerous little novels soon after 1575. Roscoe translates after the edition in 4to. *Venezia* 1609. " In many instances,'' he says (*Introd.* ibi.) " the mention of persons and of particular times and places, is introduced. It is thus he alludes to Bianca Cappello, afterwards consort of Francesco de' Medici, grand duke of Tuscany, whose nuptials were celebrated in 1579, and are very minutely described by the novelist." — It will depend upon the time when his novel was written and the place where published whether the whole story is told by Celio or not. If the above-mentioned edition was the first, we may well suppose it, for the Cardinal Grand-duke died in that year, and the volume it will be seen bears the imprint of Venice. — Meissner would seem to refer to some unedited memoir, some private scandalous chronicle, as the chief source of his materials. " Jenes berufne Manuskript von der geheimen Geschichte des Hauses Medizes, welches Orrery nutzte, und worauf Sansovino, nebst noch manchem anderm baute, mag allerdings f.r den wahren Historiker und Biographen nicht zulänglich sicher seyn; für den Halb-Roman hat es eine trefliche Eigenschaft, — Interesse." *Vorerinn.* Was this done to conceal his obligations to the Italian romancer?

(2) See subnote on p. 360 sq. Bonaventuri was killed in 1570. The Duchess Joanna died in 1578. In all that interval, a widow, besieged by the passionate assiduities of a royal lover, and surrounded by courtly examples both of unchastity and of the indifference with which it was regarded, in an age of very general profligacy, she would have been indeed a Penelope (as *Isabella* calls her in mockery,) — no, more — if she had not yielded. But there are two sides to the story of Penelope as well as of Bianca, and some ancient writers have made the wife of Ulysses the common mistress of all her suitors. Cs. App. II, note 5.

written expressly to glorify the duchy and its petty sovereigns,(3) enters into details which waken more than incredulity, and few thoughtful persons can rise from his discolored and distorted portraiture of the fair Venetian and his carefully toned miniature of the Cardinal Ferdinand, without a conviction that the pictures in their general effect might change places.

The Cardinal, a false brother and a bad man(4), in a family where murder and incest were familiar crimes, had cast a longing eye on the grand-ducal crown, which the physical infirmity of his brother's spouse made it more than probable would one day be his own. When Bianca, by no other means that I can see or suppose, than the magic of her beauty and her manners, ascended the throne as the legitimate successor of Joanna, all his schemes seemed to be blown to the winds.

(3) And written under the patronage and by the command, as he himself expresses it, of the then reigning monarch, a younger son of the House of Austria, whose lofty name he puts upon the very title-page, withholding reverently his own. The favor of this prince (Peter-Leopold, afterwards Emperor of Austria,) would certainly not be forfeited by an endeavor to blacken the character of the Archduchess' rival.

And here I may as well state, in preparation for the whole of the Appendix following, that Galluzzi claims to have drawn his material exclusively from the Medicean Archives, . . *"tutte estratte fedelmente dall' Archivio Mediceo."* In the same brief advertisement, however, he alludes to the exist- nce of popular fallacies as to certain events. and tells us he enters into minuteness of detail therein, for the very purpose of correcting these errors of belief and of tradition, — of course by the *Archives.* Now, are the Archives infallible? Are they, in fact, entire? or in their entirety, veritable? Would the Cardinal have been likely to leave anything that would tend to inculpate him in the matter of Bianca and the Grand-duke, or not to give prominence as well as permanence to inventions which would account morally for his detestation of the former, and palliate, with most men, the atrocity of his unchristian and unprincely efforts to blacken for ever her memory? He had the power to tamper with the Archives, and he was not a man to leave it unused. Consult, in Appendix 11., Note 12, also 19.

(4) See below, in Note 15, what Sismondi says of him.

16*

And when finally, as Grand-duchess, she was about to become a mother, he resolved to rid himself by one blow of both obstacles to his ambition. Bianca's great weakness, as well as doubtless one of her principal attractions, seems to have been a benevolent amiability. She did her best at all times to reconcile her lord with the Cardinal, whose profligate intrigues and importunate avarice had alienated his ducal brother. And she succeeded only too well. The Cardinal is invited to a banquet. He refuses to partake of the blancmange which was his inviter's favorite dish, and when both Bianca and the Grand-duke, after eating freely of it, are seized at the very table with pangs that denoted poisoning, he prevented all assistance from being rendered to either, had them shut up indeed in a disfurnished and gloomy chamber of the villa, and took measures even before their death to secure possession of the fortresses and put down by armed force any attempts that should be made to prevent his becoming master of the city.(5) Proclaiming loudly that the Duke and Duchess had attempted to poison him and by mistake had swallowed their own bane, he retracted this absurd invention by declaring there was no poison in the case at all, that the Duke and Duchess had both died of a surfeit.(6) As this story was more absurd, if possible, than the other, since the deaths were nearly simultaneous, and the preceding symptoms had indicated some sudden and violent action upon the vitals, he had the bodies opened. Now at that day science had not advanced so far as to make the detection of the secret administration of poisons, especially if of a vegetable origin, in all cases possible. Indeed even at the present time, it is known, and we have authority for the assertion, that there are venene substances whose operation cannot be traced after death.(7) And this must be particularly the case, to ocular in-

---

(5) There was no hesitancy on his part. The commander of the citadel at Leghorn showing some unwillingness to acknowledge his authority, the Cardinal had him hung. See Appendix II., Note 24.

(6) See Appendix II., y. 1587, second paragraph.

(7) I have mislaid a newspaper quotation from a lecture by our townsman Prof.

spection, where the poison has been slow in its effects, because, in the first place, of its probable elimination from the system,(8) and, secondly, of the liability to confound its indications with those of natural disease. Now, if the account which Galluzzi gives of the *tertian fever* with its *vehement thirst*(9) which seized the Duke and Duchess so sin-

Doremus, bearing directly upon this point. But it will be sufficient to cite the following, in respect to metallic poisons, which can be traced : —

. . . "It is known, that three or four grains of arsenic, a quantity *insufficient to produce any striking local changes*, will destroy a person under all the usual symptoms of poisoning by this substance. The same may be said of corrosive sublimate : — three or four grains of this poison *would suffice to kill an adult; and yet*, from this small quantity, *the local changes would be barely perceptible*." TAYLOR, *On Poisons in relat. to Med. Jur.* &c. (Phil. ed. 8°. 1848) p. 27. And again : "That death should ever take place in poisoning, without any physical changes being produced on the body, is not more wonderful than that it should occur under attacks of tetanus or hydrophobia, in which diseases, as is well known, no post-mortem appearances are met with sufficient to account for their rapidly fatal course." (*Ib.*)

But this is still more complete :

. . . "To take arsenic as an example, — *if the dose has been small, and the person has survived* the effects *for a certain period, it is not likely that the poison will be detected* in the soft organs of the body. *The deceased may have survived long enough for the whole of the poison to be expelled.* According to Briand, *after ten, twelve, or fifteen days, not a particle of arsenic* or tartarized antimony *will be discovered* in the bodies of animals poisoned by either of these substances. (*Ib.* p. 30.) See further on same page.

The subject is resumed in Append. II., Note 22.

(8) As I have shown in Note 7. Briand gives *ten, twelve*, and *fifteen days* for the complete disappearance of the poison. Orfila himself (*Traité de Toxicol.* 5° éd. Paris, in 8°.; t. 1. p. 427) assigns *from twelve to fifteen*. The Grand-duke survived *eleven* and Bianca *ten days*, — according to the *Archives*.

(9) See, in Appendix II., y. 1557, and footnote. — The Cardinal Ippolito de' Medici was affected similarly, and died after four days' illness ; that is, according to Varchi ; but six, as I compute it: for he was attacked on the 5th of August and expired on the 10th, (1535.) The moment after he had eaten the broth in which

gularly, and so conveniently for the Cardinal, within two days of each
other, and terminated, with an interval of a single day, in the death

the poison was conveyed, the Cardinal began to suffer. He grew rapidly worse,
" and went on wasting little by little and having *continually a very slight and
slow fever.*" (*Stor. Flor.* v. 131, 132.) He was poisoned, as some supposed, by
his cousin Duke Alexander(a), as others, by Pope Paul III.(b) That most fear-

(a) The most probable hypothesis. And if what Segni appears inclined to believe, although he cites the
story merely as a rumor of the day, be true, viz., that Ippolito had previously tried to blow up the Duke with
gunpowder (vol. ii. p. 85), the latter might, if the rumor were current before the death of Ippolito, have satisfied his own conscience by the supposition of its truth, if afterward, he might himself have originated it as
an offset to his own atrocity. One scarcely knows what to hold to, in so contradictory accounts ; but such a
crime, besides that it is plausible to attribute the attempt to the known political enemies of Alessandro, who
were many of them zealous but not over-scrupulous friends of liberty, one of whom finally effected his assassination, such a crime is inconsistent with the character of the young Cardinal, who, though passionately
ambitious, and openly resentful of the injustice done him in the elevation of his junior, Alexander, had
nothing in his impetuous, candid, and generous character which allows us to impute to him the design of a
coward and a murderer. Unfit to be a churchman, partial, almost ostentatiously, to arms and to the chase
(see *Appendix* III.), he led the life of a gay but not dissipated prince, and died, according to Segni himself,
with unaffected piety and with the modest charity of a Christian — as a Christian should be. This local
historian tells us, very differently from Varchi, that the ill-fated young man expired in thirteen hours after
the attack, and that two of his friends died subsequently ; for, according to Segni, instead of the Cardinal's
being indisposed and in bed when the poisoned broth was brought to him, he and his friends *were supping
together gaily at Itri.* — Such is history ; Varchi, writing under Cosmo, and Segni under his successor ; yet,
in so tragical an incident, varying both as to the inception and the termination of the affair ! It is, that,
in such a case, Rumor, never perhaps single-voiced, has more than the usual number of tongues. The latter
writer continues : The friends of the Duke ascribed the murder to Pope Paul, "come quegli che, desideroso
de' gran benefici posseduti da lui per dare al Card. Farnese, l' avesse in questo modo fatto morire." Some
indeed ascribed the event to the pestilential air (as Bianca and Francesco's death was attributed to intermittent fever.) Segni considers it the truest and most certain report, which lays it at the door of Duke
Alexander. (*Ib.* 83, sq.)

(b) *Alessandro da Farnese, Cardinal d' Ostia,* — who succeeded Clement VII. in that chair whose existence
still remains, but will probably not much longer, the opprobrium of human sense and of manhood, and should
make a Christian blush to throw imposture in the teeth of Mohammedans, — the so-called seat of St. Peter,
who never put a round in it. According to Varchi (an historian of rare ingenuousness) Paul III. was a
finished dissembler, concealing his real vices by outward decorum and sanctity. (*Ib.* 69.) It is likely ; it
belonged to his profession and his place. He died, this man who could be suspected in his old age of raising
a cowardly assassination, to swell by misappropriation, not to say robbery, the state and splendor of his
reprobate bastard son° and of his grandchildren (see again Varchi in loc. cit. 134, 5. The detail, after his
faulty but interesting manner, is curious. Also, from p. 210 to end of the vol.) — he died, this Vicegerent of
Christ, with the words : *If my family had not ruled me, I should be stainless.* Everybody remembers what
Hildebrand's last words were, what Cardinal Wolsey's, what perhaps those of a dozen gallows-birds, as well
as princes of the Church, have been. When a man has lied and dissembled all his life, he will not be likely
to want a good name after death, if an additional falsehood can buy it for him. The vulgar superstition

° It is useful to my vindication of the character of Bianca, to note here another striking historial discrep-
ancy. This scapegrace, who, according to Galluzzi, *had all the vices of Duke Valentine* [Cæsar Borgia] *without his talents* (Intr. liv.), and of whom Varchi tells in detail that revolting personal outrage which ended in
the death of the gentle Bishop of Fano (S. F. ap. *finem*), is described by Segni (an intelligent as well as honest
writer) as not without learning and well able to behave himself (*Ib.* 13° · · v. lii. p. 14.) Again, on the other
hand, his father, Paul III., who, Eli-like, encouraged his prodigacy by his criminal indifference or impolitic
leniency, was, according to the first-named author, *a man of rare talents and of extraordinary sagacity !* (*Ib.*
liii.) I wish to enforce on the reader's sense these continual dissonances in judgment and in fact-record,
and must be pardoned for a little irrelevancy.

of both, be correct(10), the former was eleven days suffering, and the
latter ten, and the difficulty of detection would be very greatly increased. Besides, these investigators, if they were such (for there is
no mention of anything more than the opening of the bodies and a

ful, because least evitable, mode of assassination, which in the beginning of the
century had flourished under the auspices and with the coöperation of the Holy
See, was still horribly familiar to the great. Francesco himself was suspected of
practising it, and Cosmo was, as mentioned in the text, accounted "a subtle
poison-mixer." (See Appendix II. *ad init.*) Varchi has several stories of the
kind, as *e. g.*, besides that of the Cardinal Ippolito, the remarkable one of the
beautiful Luisa Strozzi, wife of Luigi Capponi, poisoned by her own relatives on
mere suspicion of the likelihood of her falling a victim to the libertinism of
Duke Alessandro (v. 104–106), but according to Segni by the Duke himself, because she had refused to yield to his desires(c). *Storie Fior. l. 7°.* (vol. II. p.
65, sq. ed. Mil. 1805, in 8°.)

(10) But I have argued that the record of the Medicean Archives cannot in the
story of Bianca be accepted as correct and is not likely to be even truthful. *Note*
(3): also various places in *Append. II.* It is said that in the Introduction of the
work cited in Append. II. Note 4, Miss Strickland, on the authority of Evelyn, accuses Burnet of destroying historical autographs. Yet the Bishop of Sarum was
both a good man and a virtuous prelate. The Cardinal Grand-duke was neither,
even in the eyes of Sismondi, and he hated Bianca with a hatred which he took
no pains to conceal. Append. II. *pr. finem.*

which believes that in the death-hour nothing can be uttered but the truth is a convenient one, nor will either
Paul III. be the last vicious personage, nor Elizabeth Surratt the last convict, whose final declaration will be
accepted by a partial historian, or be availed of by a cunning barrister, as evidence of innocence.

(c) Yet Segni, whose honesty as a writer is unquestioned, claims for such a monster, who he tells us (ii p
50) corrupted even the sacred virgins and committed in the very sanctuary (like the diabolical Pope John
XII., or the corsair-pope, the 23rd of that pontifical name) "assai vergogne nefande ", both abilities and
good dispositions, and attributes (*this* unphilosophically, if not absurdly) his immeasurable licentiousness to
evil counsels. It had been more rational to ascribe it to the gift of his mother, aided by that profligate in
purple the Cardinal Giulio — or by the Cardinal's coachman. But in conclusion he admits, that he was "universally hated ", because, notwithstanding his even-handed justice, high courage, and resolute will, " he had
withal acquired the name of cruel, of voluptuous and impious, to such a degree that he had become an object
of disgust to everybody." (lib. 6°. *prope init.*) All of which furnishes one of many instances of the difficulty which attends the search for truth in history.

I may add, as being of interest and not ungerman to my text, what Segni has to say of Alexander's illegitimacy. It appears that a third party, as I have just hinted, might have put in a claim for priority with the
two Medici. . . "Alessandro de' Medici, il quale era figlio naturale di Lorenzo, nato d' una schiava chiamata
Anna, la quale avendo avuto ancora che fare con Giulio Priore di Capua e poi Papa Clemente, ed ancora con
un vetturale, che tenevano in casa quando erano ribelli, era incerto di chi fosse figliuolo." (l. i. ed. cit. p. 105.

simple inspection of the viscera,) would understand it was the Cardinal's pleasure they should not find anything to confirm suspicion,
and it would have been a miracle of independence and moral courage
had they dared under the circumstances to disappoint him.(11)   Here
the infamy of this vile churchman does not end.   Giving orders for
the sumptuous burial of his brother, he had Bianca thrown upon the
common heap of bodies of the abandoned poor and vicious.   This
might have been done to confirm in men's minds the opinion he had
diligently disseminated of her utter worthlessness and of his disgust
and hatred of an adventuress and "sorceress" who had dishonored
temporarily his family.   But there was something more than this in
his conduct ; it evinced a rage that was savagely vindictive ; the rage
of a bad man who had been more than disappointed, who was conscious that he had betrayed himself and hated the involuntary posses-
sor of his degrading secret.   In short I believe, that, as I have painted
him, and the romancers before me, the Cardinal had offered love to
his brother's wife (it was quite in the mode of the family) and to his
dismay been rejected.   The indications of this doubly criminal passion
can not have escaped historians.   The Capello family, one of the rich-
est and most distinguished noble houses in Venice, was as good as
the Medici in its origin, and the Venetian Republic in its desire to
exalt Bianca (which it would not have shown — despite the insinu-
ation of Botta(12) – were her life infamous) had made her Queen of

(11) In the case of the Cardinal Ippolito, the body after death became discolored,
and, on opening it, the omentum (caul) was found corroded.   But his household
were interested in finding the traces of poison.   Those who performed the like
operation on Francesco and Bianca were interested in not finding such evidence,
and the examination on their part was probably one for form, as on the part of
the Cardinal Duke it was a challenge to the suspicion of his enemies.   See Appendix II. Note 22.

(12) Who, as an historian, should have had knowledge enough of humanity to
understand what was going on everywhere around him.   A change of fortune for
the better obliterates at once, or at least veils over for the time being, all previous

Cyprus. Thus put on a par with the Grand-duke, what plea could the Cardinal have found for making that immeasurable distinction between them after their common death ?(13) In the rage of his hatred, this prince of the Christian Church furnished one of the very best facts in evidence of a criminal passion whose repulse had outraged his extravagant pride and wounded past cure a self love which was the most vital part of his spirit.

Like Philip II. of Spain, and, I may add, Henry VIII. of England, the Grand-duke Ferdinand of Tuscany is represented with smooth face and fair and effeminate features. They were the mask of a character which had the revengeful malice, the remorseless cruelty, the treacherous cunning and hypocrisy, and the immeasurable ambition of a bad and masculine woman.(14)

And yet this man made a wise, a politic, and even, it is said, just sovereign.(15) The case is not singular either in Europe or in the

disadvantages, and when Botta sneers at the eagerness with which both the Capello family and the Venetian Republic made haste to acknowledge and to glorify the adventuress as Grand-duchess whom as a fugitive they had proscribed and proclaimed for punishment, he forgets one of the commonest of the traits of the human character. Would he not himself have found splendor in the risen sun if its rays fell on his stand-place, or would he have got out of its warmth in winter? The dogs are wiser, and the moth, though it rushes to its own destruction, has a better instinct. I affirm that Bianca's family acted in both instances precisely as every other family would have acted, and were in neither position mean or unreasonable.

(13) If it be said, because he held her to be worthless, the "pessima Bianca" he afterwards declared her (v. Append. II. ap. fin.), then his brother should have shared the same fate, and their common father before them. Where was Isabella buried?

(14) All of which traits happen to have been the moral features, ugly to deformity, of the Medici in general.

(15) Sismondi says, and well, of Ferdinand: "He had as much talent for government as one can have without virtue, and as much pride as one can preserve without nobleness of soul." Rép. it. (Paris, 1840, in 8°.) t. x. p. 227. We have seen (p.

East. The Mogul Emperor, Aurungzebe, attained the throne on which he sat so nobly, by the murder of more than one brother.

August 16, 1861.

II.

Being extracts from memoranda taken during the preparation for Acts III., IV., and V., with additions and comments subsequently made.

Cosmo bore the reputation of being a subtle maker of poisons ; Y. 1574. and it is certain he endeavored to destroy Strozzi by them. But Strozzi did the same for him. GALLUZ. *Granduc.* ii. 185. The historian's language is positive : " E *certo* che egli tentò di usarne contro lo Strozzi." Yet observe the high character which he gives to Cosmo, after this charge and the assertion that his criminal laws, founded on the Spanish maxims then prevalent in all Italy, *were absolutely destitute of every sentiment of humanity*, and "egli venerava le istruzioni e i consigli dei suoi congiunti Vice Rè Don Pietro di Toledo(1) e Duca d' Alva, che furono i due più sanguinari Ministri che abbino conculcato l' umanità " (*ib.*) ; and then see to what amounts the like charge against Francesco. Sismondi, who says that Cosmo

373, subnote *c*) that *even-handed justice* is assigned to that infamous profligate, Duke Alexander. Here are the very words of Segni, and in detail : "le quali [*sc.* le faccende pubbliche] . . . egli amministrava da sè stesso con grand' animo e con molta risoluzione, ed avrebbe soddisfatto in gran parte alla giustizia, perchè la faceva al piccolo come al grande, ed udiva volentieri le povere genti, se i piaceri giovenili nell' avessono distratto pur troppo da questi consigli, ec." Stor. Fior. *lib.* 6°, t. ii. p. 19.

(1) This D. Pietro di Toledo, Viceroy of Naples, confessed in 1550 to a Secretary of Duke Cosmo's, that, after his possession of the government, there perished in the single city of Naples by the hands of justice *eighteen thousand persons.* Granduc. *Introd.* p. 2.

had established a manufactory of poisons in his palace under the pretence of making chemical experiments, (the passage is quoted under y. 1578,) is more consistent, although we shall see that in his summing-up of the character of Francesco, he contradicts not only Galluzzi, but certain facts which do not depend upon the allegations of historians. And Botta, we shall find, does just the same. See note 20.

A year after the death of Cosmo. — The conspiracy against 1575. Cosmo, and for which Pandolfo Pucci had atoned with his life in 1560, was renewed against his successor, and by the son of this very Pucci, Orazio, whom the Grand-duke by numerous benefits had endeavored in vain to make forget his father's merited execution. [Here again Galluzzi gives a trait that does not agree with his picture of Francesco. See under 1578.] The Cardinal at Rome learning of the plot informed Francesco of it [which Galluzzi considers generous, although, as the conspiracy was directed in the name of the ancient liberty against the whole reigning family, he was to have been one of the victims,] and advised the arrest of Pucci. About twenty youths in all were complicated, and the confiscations amounted to 30,000 ducats. This severity and the fiscal exactions irritated the people and rendered hostile all the connections of the young nobles. *Granduc.* ii. 248.

Masnade [bands of predatory soldiers, brigands or assassins according to circumstances, and serving as instruments both of rapine and revenge] increased fearfully ; the nobles having them in pay for their fends and vengeance. *Ib.* 265. — Sismondi writes in relation to the extent of brigandage after 1563 (the year of Bianca's arrival in Florence) : Alfonso Piccolomini, Duke of Monte Marciano, and Marco Sciarra, in Romagna, the Abbruzzi, and the Campagna of Rome, commanded several thousands of men. *Répub. Ital.* t. 10, p. 218 sq.

The administration of the criminal laws frightened the innocent 1576. as much as the guilty, and flattered the powerful with hopes of easily eluding them. " Quindi è che le risse, le prepotenze e gli

assassinamenti crebbero a dismisura." In eighteen months from
the death of Cosmo, there were counted in Florence alone one hundred and eighty cases of deaths and wounds by assault. *Granduc.* ii.
265.

Don Pietro de' Medici profligate and depraved. His beautiful wife
Eleonora di Toledo imitated him. Her brother refused to listen to his
complaints, and prevented their reaching Don Garzia her father. The
Spanish chivalry put the husband up to avenge his dishonor, and he
murdered her by night, July 11, with repeated blows of his poniard, at
Caffagiolo, an ancient villa of the Medici (*ib.* 267.) Her death attributed to disease of the heart.

Isabella, both beautiful and accomplished. Favored the amours of
her brother with Bianca. Duke, her husband, especially jealous of his
own kinsman Troilo Orsini; strangles her with a cord at his villa of
Correto on the morning of the 16th July. Court informed that she
fell dead in the arms of her attendants while washing her head (*ib.*
269.) — Botta tells us that Troilo himself killed with his own hand the
Grand-duke's page, between whom and this licentious princess there
was a mutual passion. The picture given by this last modern historian, of the two royal ladies, D. Pietro and, united with the godly
group, Duke Cosmo, is done with that relish with which he seems to
paint extreme depravity in high places, sparing no feature, and height-
ening without mercy the ugliness of all. Let me make a copy of the ori-
ginal, as certain touches will not bear transferring to an English panel.
" *Eleonora* . . " giovane graziosa e di maravigliosa bellezza. Corsero
romori, e ne fu anche fatto fede dalle cronache contemporanee, che
Cosimo, invaghito di tanta bellezza, con scellerato amore si fosse con
esso lei mescolato, per modo che gravida di sè alle nozze del figliuolo
la mandasse. D. Pietro poi oltraggiava i due sessi, l'altro abbandonando
e del proprio abusando.(2) Infame tresche erano queste, nè anco

(2) Cosmo, who affected a regard for morality and for religion, or better had a
politic respect for both, enacted laws of great severity against this revolting vice
and against the sin of blasphemy. (It is Segni who classes them thus together in

celate : il pubblico lo sapeva, s' aggiungeva lo scandalo al misfatto.
Pietro frequentava i bei giovani ; Eleonora prestò l' orrechio a chi la
vagheggiava." *Stor. d' Ital.* Libr. 14°. (Milano, in 12°, 1843. t. iii.
p. 166.) "Delizia della Corte e quasi fiore di Firenze per gioventù,
bellezza, grazia, ornamento di poesia, perizia di musica, moltiplicità
di favelle era donna Isabella de' Medici, figliuola del Duca Cosimo.
Ma tali sorti di fiori nella Medicea Corte si contaminavano e si lasciavano
contaminare." [The reader will please recall what I observed of
Bianca, surrounded by and inhaling such an atmosphere of moral corruption. But in the instance of Isabella the "flower" shriveled and
blackened by no outward influence of the elements ; it had destruction
at its core. The egg of the caterpillar was deposited before the germ
had begun to develop itself on the parent plant. It was the pernicious
blood of the Medici in Cosmo, and haply, on the mother's side, of the
Toledo.(3) Observe what follows.] "Portò la fama che Cosimo

the same sentence.) But the law fell into disuse from the indifference of the
magistrates, — perhaps from their knowledge to what degree this unmentionable
bestiality prevailed among the highest order. Pandolfo Pucci was one of those
who thus sinned against nature, and did it without any particular concealment
("*sfacciatamente.*") It seems he knew what to calculate upon. Through the
influence of his brother Ruberto, lately made Cardinal by Paul III., he was pardoned. But Giov. Bandini, for the same classical atrocity, was kept in a dungeon
at the bottom of a tower for nineteen years, — rather, as Segni thinks and well, for
his abusive words of the Duchess Madama Leonora than for the crime. *Stor.*
Flor. ed. cit. ii. 272.

(3) Cosmo, who, according to honest Segni, was censurable for the same sub-
servience to the Emperor(a) that Galuzzi accuses Francesco of towards the King

(a) "Non faceva altro che intratenersi per amico e per buon suddito (per parlar meglio) dell' Imperadore."
(ii. 255.) The language, in its sense, not tone, is forcible. — So also in the matter of his nuptials, this pattern
Cosmo, — who, by the by, Segni, who must have been aware of the niceties and morality recounted in an after
age by Botta, tells us "nel viver suo era molto onesto," (ib. 270,) — celebrated them with great magnificence,
although a famine was prevailing at the time, occasioned chiefly by his own avarice, — "cagionata dal tem-
porale, e molto più dall' aver l' anno innanzi il Duca dato la tratta a'grani, de' quali cavò scudi 60,000, e
sercò tutti i grani del dominio." (Ib. 215, sq.) Thus in both these instances, of a degrading policy and an
extravagance of pomp which mocked the necessities of his people, and insulted their sufferings, the great
Cosmo set the example which his son and successor is reproached for having followed. That this was so does
not excuse the latter, but it makes the censure of the historians in his precisely parallel case if not malevolent,
yet altogether partial. And it is for this reason that I have cited these instances of selfish and ignoble error

stesso troppo più l' amasse che a padre si conveniva." (*Ib.* 167.)
Who has not heard the story of the artist, who from his scaffolding
beheld —— The Cardinal's words of soliloquy in Act IV. Sc. 4 are
gloss enough in English.

For thirteen years the Duke had been enamored of Bianca, with a
passion growing every day more ardent. Nothing too good for her:
palaces, delightful gardens, *etc.*, *etc.* — his very brothers paying her
court — sole dispenser of favors. A Jewish woman said to assist her
in incantations and the composition of philters to increase the Duke's
passion. But let me quote, as I wish to examine this point in full.
After indulging in the expression "orgogliosa impudenza della Cappello" (*haughty impudence of the Capello,*) — to which on the succeeding page he adds *black perfidy* ("nera perfidia,") Galluzzi proceeds in this fashion: "La Bianca, cui troppo premeva sempre più
accenderlo e mantenerlo costante, non risparmiava veruno di quelli
artifizi che son comuni alle *femmine del suo carattere,* senza omettere
l' uso dei filtri, dei prestigi, e di tutto ciò che la credulità donnesca(4)
ha saputo imaginare d' inganni in tal genere; una donna Giudea era
la fedele ministra di questi incantesimi, e il pubblico che imaginava i

of Spain, espoused at his suggestion, instead of the Archduchess he aspired to,
Leonora di Toledo, sister of that very Viceroy of Naples whose atrocious inhumanity is cited in note (1). She brought him a son or a daughter every year.
As D. Pietro married the daughter of D. Garzia, who was brother to this lady, it
follows that in the person of his wife he poniarded also his cousin-german.

(4) The E. of Bothwell had certainly nothing *womanish* in his composition,
though much that was devilish, yet we find him on his death-bed making a confession of having used "witchcraft" (*prestigi*) and "sweet-water" (*filtri*) to excite
the Queen's affections. See Miss Strickland's *Letters of Mary Q. of Scots,* etc.
Vol. III. I have been unable to procure a copy, and cite from a newspaper re-
view of 1843. Mary was the contemporary of Bianca. The *credulity* we might
say was that of the age, did we not know what is going on in our own skeptical
century, and in our matter-of-fact country, not to speak of France, where, succeeding to the spiritualism of Home, a common soldier of Jewish origin performs the
miracles on sick and lame and blind attributed to Christ.

più stravaganti mezzi per eseguirli *concepiva sempre più del orrore per il di lei perverso carattere.*" (*Ib.* 271.) Now let us hear what Botta says : " Bianca Capello, nata al mondo *per mostrare la potenza degli attrativi femminili* [observe throughout the parts I have italicized], e la laidezza di un uomo a cui era da Dio comandato non solo di governare, [I cannot see that Heaven had anything to do with it ; the government of the Medici was, as Botta himself has shown, an absolute usurpation founded in perfidy and corruption, and the family that administered it, from Alessandro down, were mostly worthless as princes and despicable or detestable as men,] ma di edificare un popolo atto ad ogni gentil creanza, [Varchi, who knew them better, being of them, in the reign of Cosmo, has ascribed to the Florentines no such aptitude,] fuggiva nel 1563, *ec. Bella e spiritosa e di grazie moltiformi dotata* (imperciocchè o *che scherzasse, o sopra sè stesse, o il leggiadro volto con sembianza di mestizia annuvolasse, sempre risplendeva in lei un cotal lume di avvenenza lusinghiera, di vaghezza ghiotta, che l' uom rapiva*) aveva, *ec.*" (*ubi cit.* p. 169.) Yet after this description of a beauty and grace that must have been all but irresistible and that he himself affirms *transported everybody*, — a description which, if we may judge by one trait, the " vaghezza ghiotta" (*charms that kindled appetite*), easily discernible in her portraits, (*v.* App. III.), is a faithful, though a lovely picture. — he pretends to say she had recourse to philters and to incantations to increase the passion of a man not yet forty ! However, of that presently. — The historian, with his usually sarcastic and often terrible pen, tells us that their loves were shamelessly open. " Non sentivano vergogna nell' amore : in fronte del popolo con modi scoperti il Principe il confessava, impudicizia ed impudenza regnavano.(5) Cosimo l'ammoniva" —— a precious mon-

(5) I ask again, if their loves were so impudently shameless, how came it that, after the death of Joanna, Bianca was admitted to the palace under the plea of guardianship for the young princesses, and why the secret marriage ? These facts cannot be reconciled, as before observed (p. 360,) with open impudicity.(a)—But

(a) In that place, it is true, I expressed more than a doubt of my heroine's chastity in her widowhood. It seemed to me at the time incredible, that even the Cardinal in his "declaratory act" should have falsified

itor, even were there no Camilla! (e. Botta's own words on p. 378), —— "la principessa sposa piangeva "—— that is but supposition, a fancy family-picture, though painted with an eye to nature(6), —— "c

suppose they can; suppose the Prince did indeed unveil his passion to the public gaze; when have princes done otherwise, in every land, and to our very day? In moral, or at least morality-boasting, England, the children of lawless royal love, whether gotten on a duchess or an actress, are ennobled, and the bend sinister or *baton coupé* of the Earl or Duke stands not in the way of lawful marshaling by pale or quarter with the proudest escutcheons. But in Italy! and at that time! when half the petty thrones were filled by bastards, and where, not forty years before, the child of three fathers, begotten on a wanton householddrudge, was the first acknowledged sovereign of the "Illustrissima Casa"! *Galimatias!*

(6) Not because the princess-spouse bewept his infidelity, for she knew that offence was common with all princes, but because she felt it a reproach to her own ill-favored visage, its pallor, and her dwarfish form. The whole picture, including the monitions of the saintly Cosmo, is drawn from models of the imagination, and is what the reader has been familiar with in the nursery:

> "In vain his father's kind advice,
> In vain his mother's care," *etc.*

I have no idea of apologizing for incontinence, much less adultery; but I do maintain that had Francesco been guilty of nothing worse than seeking solace with the widow Bonaventuri, he would be judged at least as leniently as his contemporary and posthumous son-in-law, that darling of all true hearts, the great Henry IV. of France, who, but for his Minister, would have committed the same folly as Francesco (if in Francesco it was a folly to marry Bianca), and who, had he not had that Minister, but a false and aspiring brother to shape for men his reputation, might have come down to us in more questionable form, his vices all exaggerated, and his frank, generous and valiant heart shrunken under their swollen heap to a pitiful littleness. As it was, it is observable that the most mischievous aspersion of his character came from the pen of his blood-relation the Princess of Conti.(a)

the date as well as other particulars of D. Antonio's birth. But when I consider what appears to have been done in the account of the Duke and Bianca's illness, I see no good reason why, in the very face of the people, that arch-maligner should not misrepresent the print of time in one case as well as in the other. See (21); also subnote to (6).

(a) The handsome and talented Louisa-Margaret of Lorraine (granddaughter of that magnanimous and valiant captain, Francis of Lorraine, Duke of Guise) in her *Histoire des Amours du grand Alcandre*, which

gli dava esempio d' ogni virtu "——what were they? She could not
but of chastity, or she were as foul as her sister-in-law, who was neither pallid, nor diminutive, nor ill-favored, to render chastity easy, ——
" ma nulla giovava, perchè la Bianca, col suo volto, *non so se mi debba
dire angelico o diabolico*, era più forte del padre, della moglie, e di
quanto il mondo pensasse o dicesse." (*ib.* 170, sq.) All of which is
merely rhetorical. And now for the absurd story of the philters, and
told thus absurdly : " *Oltre le grazie della persona* —— And what were
these *physical attractions, besides* which, *etc. ? Beautiful and spiritual
and endowed with manifold graces* (these are his own words, above
quoted,) — *since, whether she was mirthful or grave, or clouded her
elegant and charming visage with a semblance of sadness, there always
shone out in her such a light of seductive attractions, of appetible beauty*,

And who does not know what that very Minister, that virtuous Sully, whose friendship as well as administration honored both reciprocally, who does not know what
he has told of the effect of Henry's amours, leading him, as they do every man,
the honest and the good not excepted, into subterfuge and even falsehood? Un-
happily for Francis-Mary, he had not what the historian of the Medicean duchy
assigns him, *every quality that is desirable in a sovereign*. Had he had, and
been *gracious and benevolent to his subjects*, he might have said at least what
Henry said, who said most things wittily and well : " I am myself the best assur-
ance for my people. My predecessor feared you and loved you not ; but I love
you, and I have no fear of you." And in that case History would have looked,
though sorrowfully, yet gently on his vices of habit and temperament, over-
shadowed as they were by those of Henry, both an inveterate gamester and, to the
very last, incorrigible — I cannot say libertine ; it is not a word that suits a
man like him, who probably found women lewd, not made them so ; but -- to
his latest day intemperate woman-lover.

bears the same satirical relation to the Court of Henry IV. as Bussi's *H stoire amoureuse* to the not less
licentious one of Louis XIV. She too in her widowhood made, like Bianca, what the French call *a marriage
of conscience* with one of her lovers, the famous Marshal Bassompierre : a fact worth noticing as tending to
confirm by similitude of instance what, notwithstanding the brand of illegitimacy put upon Don Antonio, was
perhaps the true state of things between the G. Duke and Bianca. Bianca was too scrupulous, or too proud,
or too artful, whichever you will, to submit to his embraces except after a secret ceremony which satisfied
the conscience. Unless it was performed from a moral and religious motive, or to cover her good name, I
cannot see what was the use of such a rite. The public espousals could not in decency take place two months
after the death of Joanna, but the secret nuptials did.

as ravished the beholder —— "Oltre le grazie della persona, usava Bianca, per fomentare la passione del Granduca, i filtri, i prestigi ed il ministerio di una Giudea, cui il mondo credeva esperta d' incantesimi, ed era veramente d' inganni. La fattuchiera [*sorceress*] era *Bianca*, non la Giudea." (*ib.* 171.) Thus, either from Galluzzi (for he uses the same expressions), or directly from those Cardinalized archives which awakened no suspicion with the former, we have Botta repeating with emphasis this puerile story, without at all being conscious that in ascribing to Bianca such marvelous beauty and such entrancing manners, he makes it nearly impossible, whatever her self-delusion as to the actuality of sorcery, that she could have resorted to its fallacious assistance. What would be the object? If she already held the Duke a slave to the double enchantment of her person and her mind, — and Galluzzi tells us that his passion was continually increasing, — where was the need of anything beyond ("oltre")? And *philters!* for whom? The Duke on the day of his death was but forty-seven years of age, or forty-nine, computing after Segni(7); and Botta is

---

(7) Who tells us Francesco was nine years old when sent to meet at Genoa the Emperor's son Don Philip (afterwards Philip II. of Spain). And this was in the year 1547. — *St. Fior.* t. ii. p. 379.

It has not escaped me, that the historians may mean that Bianca plied these arts to keep the Duke from inconstancy. Indeed Galluzzi says as much (*sup.* 380). and Muratori tells us, after a contemporary, that in the popular rumor which ascribed the poisoning to Bianca, she was thought to have been urged by jealousy, being " a woman of proud spirit." See *infra* 27. The Duke was then no longer under her influence. Where then was his infatuation, or what was become of Bianca's power? If they still existed, then she had no need of drugs and magic charms; if they did not, and he became her slave to the degree which we shall shortly see asserted, then his chains were forged by magic, and the eyes of the *angelic visage* "rained influence " by the drugs!

In fact, nothing can be more contradictory than the accounts of both historians. Galluzzi, besides his prejudice, is blinded by the Cardinal Grand-duke's Archives; Botta is guided by that satiric spirit and prejudgment which see evil rather than good and find a delight in making the picture more effective by its shadows, although

writing of a period eleven years earlier (1576). He was consequently at that time but thirty-six or at most but thirty-eight years old ; and if Bianca's sorcery was so notorious as to fill the city with horror, the Duke must have known of it. Are we to suppose then, that in the full vigor of his best manhood he suffered such practices ? If he had occasion for them, then his passion could not have gone on increasing ; for love the least sensual, as the most of it is wholly so, diminishes under such circumstances, if it does not become at once extinct. As for Bianca herself, we are told it was in 1563 that she fled from Venice. Supposing she was then eighteen,—though I would rather believe she was two or even three years younger, for women at eighteen are not so easily led astray by a first passion as when its stimulus is still a new and almost uncontrollable sensation, —supposing her to be eighteen at that period, she was then in 1576 but thirty-one. Where then, I repeat, was the use of sorcery and love-potions to urge a man deeply enamored, himself in the flower of his manhood, to greater passion for a woman who could not have lost a beauty that was at any time reputed marvelous, and who is said to have had such ravishing grace of manner and so seductive sweetness of look, that, whatever the mood she might be in, or might assume, she transported every heart ? But, not to carry mere argument too far on a point which so little deserves it, let us adduce the force of a parallel example. About a century and a half before this time, Valentina of Milan, Duchess of Orleans, a woman like Bianca beautiful and intellectual, was said to owe her influence over her brother-in-law, the unhappy Charles VI., to sorcery. She was even obliged to forsake the Court for some time to escape the insults of the populace, who probably were stimulated by the King's uncles and their wives, as in the case of Bianca they

at the expense too often of real nature and the observation of historic truth. It is to be observed, that it was after all the villany ascribed to her by both these writers, that they chronicle the secret marriage and the subsequent grand espousals with the coronation, both of which acts are the strongest evidence that the Grand duke's passion had not abated.

were by the artifices of the Duke's brother. Calumny did not stop here, and to want of chastity in favor of the insane king added even the report of her poisoning him for the benefit of her husband !(8) But we are in the 19th century, three hundred years since Bianca lived and loved, and was adored—although we should hardly suppose it from the number of fortune-tellers who under various styles advertise the black art in the journals, — we are in an era of very general instruction and greatly increased freedom from superstition, yet what comes to us, even now while I write, from the land where the beautiful Venetian lived and was adored and finally suffered? The spread of cholera is attributed to the malignity of evil-disposed persons, and an unfortunate woman in Naples who professed to be of the trade of Bianca's Jewess is actually cut into pieces as having been instrumental in its propagation. See then the people of Florence wondering at the extent of Bianca's influence, precisely as in that earlier age the people of Paris did at the elegant Visconti's, and in their blind amazement prompted to an easy explanation after their own mode of thinking by the Cardinal's agents, and you have the story.(9) The Jewess may have been a sorceress like her ancient compatriot, but was probably some female-nostrum vender, or woman's-doctor, possessed of (or so

(8) It was the handsome, dissipated, and ambitious Louis of France, her husband, whose actual dabbling with the fallacious art gave a color of truth-likeness to these scandals. Martin calls him "adepte temeraire des arts *damnables* de la magie." *Hist. de France.* (Paris, in 8°, 1844) t. vi. p. 208. See too *ib.* p. 269. And Henry IV. of England, in the last of his despatches, did not hesitate to accuse him, not her, of causing the malady of Charles VI by *sorceries et diableries.* *Id. ib.* 301.

(9) If the people were wild with horror at Bianca's supposed practices, what protected her from their fury any more than Valentina? The fanaticism of a mob is the hideous growth of no peculiar age or country. The deformed and bloodthirsty giant was the same in the 16th as in the 14th century, and is the same in the 19th that he was in the 14th. Lola Montes was hooted and pelted in Munich, and so was her royal lover, who was neither *stupid* nor *cruel,* nor a *Medici ;* yet nobody ascribed his infatuation to anything supernatural.

claiming) secrets of embellishment and rejuvenation, a priestess of the thaumaturgy of the toilet ; but the stories set afloat are like, both in themselves and in their origin, those circulated, more than a hundred and fifty years before, against the fair and intellectual grandmother of Louis XII.(10)   In fine, if Bianca was the victim of the self-delusion ascribed to her, her practices under it were to increase or secure the affections of her husband, of infidelity to whom there is not breathed against her even a suspicion.   It is rather remarkable that while unwilling to ascribe the Grand-duke's excessive passion for Bianca to anything but her nefarious arts (how many would be glad to know them !) there is no thought of attacking Camilla Martelli for a like infatuation on the part of Cosmo, — Cosmo, the strong-minded,

(10) In Bianca's day, the belief in magic was still prevalent even among the educated. Not to cite again the credulity of Bothwell (who was however little more than a rude soldier), that popinjay of a king, yet gallant cavalier, half woman, half man, Henry III. of France, ashamed of his fantastical grief for Mary of Clèves, Princess of Condé, ascribed its excesses to enchantment. This was about the very period now in question, while, twenty-two years earlier, books on astronomy and geometry had actually been condemned in England as treatises of magic, notwithstanding the advances made there as elsewhere in both those sciences.

In the intervening age between Valentina and Bianca, or about a century before the latter's empoisonment, we find the usurper-Richard laying his withered arm to the witchcraft of unhappy Shore. And less than a score of years after the latter, or in the first decade of the 17th century, Mary Stuart's son, James I. of England, a man something more than educated, was a good believer in witches ; while in France Eleonora Galigaï, the foster-sister and favorite of Mary of Medici (Francesco's daughter), was put to death, although in reality for her insolent presumption and the venal abuse of her influence, yet on the charge of practising sorcery.(a) And this was about the time when Galileo stood up in the Inquisition, before the slaves of ignorance and the children of superstition, to defend by subterfuge, or by fables which he believed not, the conceptions of his God-inspired mind.

(a) It is a coincidence that the chief point in the accusation against her was that she consorted with a Jewish doctor, familiar with the art.

politic, and resolute,—who was so mastered by his love that even his physicians could not keep him from that enchantress. (GALL. ii. 176.) We now come to the "*nera prgilia*." The Duke was anxious to have male children, and rather than not have any was contented they should be illegitimate. Bianca set to work to gratify him; but her body being rendered unfruitful by sickness and dissipation ("disordini") she contrived this scheme. Three women of the vilest class (GALL.) or of vulgar standing (BOTTA), about to be confined, were engaged to part with their offspring. One of them only (providentially — in two respects) brought forth a male. This was carried, in a lute, to the bedchamber where lay the Duchess affecting, like our Mrs. Cunningham, a mother's throes. (The reader has heard of a musical instrument before as a vehicle of supposititious children to royal houses.) As the Duke was perpetually with Bianca we are told, up to the last moment, when on some pretext she sent him off, we are left to wonder by what subtilty of contrivance and by what good fortune she could deceive him as to her situation. I need not explain my meaning. Every man will comprehend it, without being read in gestation. Thus much however. A woman may feign pregnancy to strangers, but not to her husband. The "outward and visible signs" are such, that unless he were deprived of his eyes or had his arms amputated, the imposition would be impossible. Besides, the Duke in his ecstacy of expectation would have been the last man not to satisfy himself, in the innocent way that all curious expectant fathers do. I dare say he did a hundred times. (*Mensibus graviditatis jam fere exactis, superimposita pregnantis abdomini manu, motiuncula, quasi foetus tantillum subsultantis, sensibilis creberrime fiet.*) But let us suppose a miracle, and that the Duke could through six months be kept away from any contact with the woman he adored. Was the Cardinal too deceived? We shall see presently how he acted upon the Duke's death. Botta however finds nothing wonderful in the transaction; for, according to him, Bianca had the effrontery to tell the Duke himself of these false pretensions and that the little Antonio was but the son of a common man and woman of the country! And the Duke,—*it was all one,*

says that historian, *for the stupid and cruel Medici* (. . fu tuttuno per
lo stupido e crudele Medici,") — was perfectly satisfied! He might
well add, in this belief, "Se Francesco fosse più vile, o Bianca più
furba, io nol saprei." (*v. cit.* p. 172). Now this *stupid Medici* (the
epithet of *cruel* was out of place in the present matter) is pronounced
by Galluzzi, in very positive language, to have been *the most accomplished as well as talented monarch of his time!*(11) Let me make then

(11) *Cs. infra* (20.) — It will there be also found, that Sismondi, like Botta, de-
prives him of all talent as well as virtue. Where does the truth lie? What becomes of his known patronage of the arts? of science? of letters? Speaking of
his taste and magnificence in the adornment of Florence, Galluzzi says : " Il gusto
particolare de erigere nuove fabbriche e riparare e ingrandire le vecchie si distinse
nel G. Duca Francesco superiormente alle altre sue inclinazioni." ii. 473 . . . .
Consequently, he continues, *the fine arts flourished with no less splendor than
in the reign of Cosmo, and elegance and good taste spread themselves every
day more and more among private citizens.* ib. 474. In the text I have
alluded to the famous Benvenuto Cellini. Galluzzi particularizes, in architecture,
Ammanato and *Buontalenti*, in painting *Allori* and l'occetti (he might have
mentioned others), and *Giovanni Bologna* in sculpture. The Grand-duke's disposition for these arts he chronicles as "singolare." 475. . . "Egli stesso, *come
intelligentissimo delle medesime,* sovente ne ragionava con gli artefici e con i
gentiluomini della sua Corte *ad oggetto d' inspirare nel pubblico il gusto di
favorirle e l' inclinazione di professarle.*" (*ib.*) To him was owing the increase
of the reputation and consequent growth of the Florentine Academy, out of which
arose by separation, as in some organic creatures the offspring from the parent, in
1582 the *Crusca.* "Allo spirito nazionale ormai indirizzato da Cosimo alla letter-
atura e alli studi si aggiungeva L' INCLINAZIONE PARTICOLARE DEL G. DUCA FRAN-
CESCO PER LE LETTERE E PER I DOTTI. *Like his father, he loved the domestic
and familiar conversation of the most esteemed* [among the learned—"i dotti "],
*and took pleasure in maintaining with the absent a confidential correspond-
ence ; and therefore he failed not to honor, succor, and protect them in their
occasions.*" . . . 477 *sq.* *The Grand-duke was versed in Natural History,
and among its branches applied himself with especial diligence to Miner-
alogy and to Metallurgy.* 478. So with Botany. — He appreciated and favored
writers of history. The two Universities of Tuscany flourished under him despite

this remark. A man may be wise, and learned, and have even knowledge of the world at large and of the female sex in particular, and
yet become the slave of passion. But, "in vain," as we are told,
"the net is spread in the sight of any bird"; and he would have
needed to be more than stupid, an idiot, a human beast, to give sanction to a trick which, apart from its disgusting wickedness, left still
the grand desire of his heart unsatisfied; for Francis wanted not an
adopted child, the product, although male, of unknown parents, but
a son of his own, and born to him by the woman he loved. And I
may say it would have been *impossible*, had Bianca revealed the truth,
that he would have sought to buy for this vulgar bantling a principal-
ity in Naples. Yet that he did this we are told by Botta, and Galluzzi
goes still further. Philip of Spain had thoughts of conferring Siena
on the strumpets-brood. Philip of Spain was not a fool, if history can
be tortured into satire to make Francesco one. What then could have
perverted his judgment, or seduced his not too easy faith (at least in
matters not religious)? Was there then any doubt as to the illegitimacy of Don Antonio? May he not have been born after the secret
marriage of the Duke, and the Archives have been made to tell another
story? The Cardinal's generosity was, to say the least, suspicious.
See (24). It was in allusion to this rumor of Philip's intention that
there occurred at first, in the scene between the Cardinal and Don
Pietro (*Act V. Sc. III.*), this passage :

> More, thou art wrong'd in the present: our sire's wealth
> Must make the nest warm for the cuckoo's brood.

the Inquisition, and, what deserves commendation, he himself *conferred, from his
own knowledge of persons and of the requirements of science, the professor-
ships.* When asked in 1581 by a monk (*Frate*) for the Chair of Philosophy in
Siena, he wrote back with his own hand that he *did not want monks in such
lectures* ("Frati in tal lezione.") H. *ad fin.*

How with such evidence before him, and by himself recorded, Galluzzi could so
far forget his own portraiture of this enlightened Prince as to libel his entire
reign, can be explained only by a want of that philosophy which with benevolence
is the joint parent of charity.

How stands this Jezebel's bastard son Antonio?
Held by the people second to the throne,
With sixty thousand ducats annual income,
Fiefs, palaces, villas. Art thou tone'd? Why so;
'Twas well reminded. Hear then this. From Spain
I learn King Philip will bestow Siena
On this same brat, who flaunts with borrow'd right
Our boasted name.

             Don P. *That is not true.*

                  Card. *Ask else*

Thy friend Dorara. Will thou not awake?

I thought the Cardinal's language would be ascribed, as I meant it, to
his evil disposition and unprincipled designs. It was the hand of an
unscrupulous enemy painting the object of his hatred with the dark-
est colors furnished by malevolence to his imagination. The passage
however had to be sacrificed, because the words of Bianca in the final
Scene,

    " I bear within me what might blast thy hopes,

      Could I but live so long to give it life,"

would have given verity to the imputation that this D. Antonio was
born before her marriage with the Duke. But with these facts, taken
from Galluzzi himself, of the extraordinary honor in which this boy
was held, and of the wealth that was heaped on him, and which it will
be seen the Cardinal Grand-duke did not take away, and of the prin-
cipality designed for him by Philip, is it possible to suppose, that, let
alone a positive illegitimacy, any such abominable transaction had
taken place as that wherewith, through the malignancy and policy
of Bianca's arch-enemy, the records have furnished Galluzzi and the
inadequately perspicacious historians who with credulity or carelessness have adopted his views?(12)

(12) And it is not impossible that history, whose record is as often made up of
falsehoods as of truths, if not oftener, has lent undesignedly its dangerous distor-
tion, to what was already counterfeit, by copying without consideration the studied
scandals of the times. What has our war of the Rebellion taught us? If, two

But let us follow the amazing story further. Bianca, who had confessed her shameless duplicity and to the great content of the stupid
Duke, yet wants to get rid of her accomplices in a secret action that
was no longer secret and whose results were satisfactory on all sides,
but the Cardinal's. So she has two of them secretly put to death and
their assistants removed by exile. But the chief person, a Bolognese
governess, is retained. By and by, she wishes to get rid of her also.
So she sends her back to Bologna; and, on the way, soldiers from
Florence set upon her, and she is mortally wounded. Her statement,
taken juridically, was to the effect that *she recognized the assassins
as Florentine soldiers and cut-throats of Bianca !*(13) This from the
lips of a dismissed servant — a woman too ! and a woman utterly unprincipled by her own confession, if, as she pretended, she had been
employed by Bianca to superintend the execution of her frauds. And
the precious document (observe !) is sent, not to Francis, but to the
Cardinal Ferdinand at Rome ! How it got into the Archives and re-
mained there, was best known doubtless to the personage in whose
behoof it was concocted, — that is, if it was more than the revengeful
malice of an unworthy servant, sent away in disgrace. Certainly, it
was a roundabout way for Bianca to take with this one woman, Bianca
the "artful" as well as "spiritual," when she had so noiselessly rid
herself of all the rest.(14)   In what court of the United States, or of

hundred years hence, some historian should have had nothing to copy from but
the atrocious calumnies of Jefferson Davis and his so-called Ministers, and should
have found confirmation of the same in the congenial malice of most of the news-
papers of Great Britain and of France, what would be the record of the Union
Government ?

(13) . . "di aver conosciuto che il suo feritore *con altri compagni* erano sol-
dati Fiorentini e sicarj della Bianca." GALL. ii. 273. — For what other purpose
did her lady use them? The Governess did not say. She must have been herself the supervisor of more iniquities than child-coinage, to be familiar with the
faces of the assassin-servants. And that simpleton Bianca, not to employ new
ones !

(14) It is not to be at all supposed that a woman of the Governess's position, if

Great Britain, is it, that such testimony would be taken as proof suffi
cient of the guilt of the suspected party, and the latter too unheard "
Yet it is precisely this ex-parte evidence that comes down to us as his-

any other, would travel from Florence to Bologna, a journey then of several days,
alone, much less at a time when the whole confines were swarming as we have
seen with freebooters. Even if without companions, she must have had a *rettu-
rale*, or a guide and attendant if riding a mule.(a)   At all events she could not
have been alone; for we are told she caused herself to be carried to Bologna, being
doubtless so far on her way thither as to be in the very midst of the masnadieri.
What became then of her companion, escort, driver, or companions? Supposing
that her murder was intended, it is evident that when one man could do the job
effectually it would hardly have been committed to more than two (for that there
were several is implied in the very words of the narrative). Yet they left her
merely wounded! She had power still to travel, and strength when she arrived to
make her deposition! This was bungling work. The truth of the story may be
conjectured to be this: — The party of which the governess made one (travelers in
those days, as now, or lately, in Italy, if they had no party, waited for their opportunity to join one, but rarely if ever journeyed by themselves) were attacked by
one of those bands of brigand-soldiers of which we have spoken as among the pests
of Francesco's inefficient reign. Shots were fired to stop the party, or because
of their resistance, as they probably traveled armed, and one of them — *archibu-
sata*(b) — struck the woman. This was a fine opportunity for revenge on her part,

(a) It was about this time that coaches began to be of anything like frequent use in traveling ; but even
then they were reserved for persons of rank, and the introduction of them was looked upon with displeasure
by sovereign princes, some of these forbidding their general employment by edict. When Segni speaks of
a " vetturale " (*vetturino*) in the story of the origin of Duke Alexander, the man's employers were princes.
Henry of Navarre, when King of France, had but one carriage, and was obliged to do without, as he said on
one occasion, when the Queen was using it.

(b) The arquebuse," the first form of the musket, was a most uncertain, as clumsy and unwieldly weapon.
Those that Philip II., of Spain, introduced into his army, required a forked rest to steady them ; and it is
reasonable to suppose that these huge matchlocks, carrying a very heavy ball, were the kind adopted by
Francesco. This adds to the absurdity of the idea of sending out assassins so armed. Poor Bianca ! they
will not allow thee even sense in thy diablery ! Fancy a band of these arquebusiers making ready to shoot a
governess, who of course stands still to accommodate them, while, perched on eminences in the various long
distances of the future, three historians are gravely taking notes ! — We see too, that with such a weapon
the probability is increased of the woman's having been wounded by accident, or by divergence of the ball.

* Webster, in his derivation of this word, is in the clouds, where he.gropes too often for a composite ety-
mon. It does not *signify* a *hook-gun*, nor for that matter a *gun* at all in the sense in which we use that word.
The " arquebuse " was the direct successor of the crossbow or arbalist (*balestra*), and therefore popularly,
inevitably I might say, took the name of *hollow* or *tube bow*. " Archibuso ; *cioè arco busio*, *ovvero bucato*,
Arco, perchè *succede alle baleste*, e a' *verretoni*, e agli *archi degli autichi*." *Abat. SALVINI.   Not. nel Tratt.*
7°. *della Ling. Tosc. del Duommattci. ed. Mil. 1807. I. 268.*

17*

tory, unsustained even on its own side by one solitary proof of actual guilt. And for this, alas, we read in life-dictionaries, some of them of great repute, of the *artful and cruel* Bianca!— Herein she is more unfortunate than her unhappy contemporary Mary Stuart, whose imputed complicity in the assassination of her husband has more than one rebutting evidence coexistent with the charge itself.(15)

even if she were not put up to her villanous aspersion by an agent of the Cardinal's, who appears to have had emissaries and secret servants everywhere.

(15) What Hallam has said of a corresponding character of the 14th century, is worth observing. "The name of Joan of Naples has suffered by the lax repetition of calumnies. * * * The charge of dissolute manners, so frequently made, is not warranted by any specific proof or contemporary testimony." *State of Europe*, etc. v. i. p. 467 (N. Y. in 8°. 1863.)

Between Joanna and Mary Stuart there is considerable resemblance, both in individual traits of person and of character and in certain conspicuous points of their histories. Each was suspected of conniving at the murder of her husband, and each confirmed the suspicion with most minds (but, I think, illogically,) by marrying the principal assassin.(a) And between all three of the personages before us, the contemporaries Mary and Bianca and their quasi-prototype of two centuries before, there is the common point of a calumniated character. Yet Joanna whom Hallam thus partially exculpates was probably the most condemnable of all three. Does not everybody know of his own experience private instances of detraction, and of misapplied accusation of crime or misconduct whereof the really guilty party escapes all censure? History is but a repetition on a large scale and before the world of what transpires in the narrow and obscure circle of familiar intercourse.

(a) This is not the place to argue such a point, but, writing for the future, I take up space to assert that a woman, who had been privy to the murder of her husband, would not, — except she were of the very lowest order of humanity and of the most degrading associations, — have consented, of free will, to marry his assassin.

Shakspeare, in a grotesquely unnatural scene, makes *Lady Anne* to be won by *Gloster* even while the usurper confesses to have killed her husband. This is natural enough in the result of his wooing, as commented on in his soliloquy, and only unnatural because of the exaggeration in brevity of time, and that lack of every consideration of propriety of language, manner, and sentiment which is a frequently occurring fault of that great poet. It is natural, I say, so far as the influence of such a suit on the mind of a vain, ambitious and weak woman; but then Anne of Warwick had not been privy nor consenting to the murder of Edward. A case absolutely to the point; for the widow of Prince Edward did marry his chief murderer. And the tyrant would have also had the Princess Elizabeth his niece, had the latter consented; for her mother was willing to betroth her to the butcher of her own three sons and of her husband. Yet none would be so mad as even to suspect Anne or the Queen Dowager of complicity in any of those assassinations.

Remember, all these foul accusations are made, not against a vulgar, ignorant, and low-minded woman, but one who by the united testimony of her worst defamers was, like Mary herself, gifted with intellect as well as beauty, and was moreover of a lofty spirit, although what to one writer is simply lofty becomes, in the vituperation of another, haughtiness and insolent presumption. Add to this, that Francis, whether "cruel" or not, was still a Medici, that he had suffered, if not sanctioned, the assassination of his own sister and of his brother's wife for their debauchery, and would hardly have endured, above all he a man not indifferent but passionately enamored, therefore liable to jealousy, and one who, according to Galluzzi, *never forgave*, any departure from chastity by Bianca. As I have said, there is no suspicion breathed against her except what may be gathered from a vague and uncertain epithet or phrase.(16) Had there been cause, a single example, the historians would not have failed to

(16) All of Galluzzi's terms and epithets show what a view he had taken of Bianca's character; and Sismondi follows him without distrust ("l'artificeuse et débauchée"); while Botta, according to his manner, with intensity of accumulative sarcasm, treats us to this extraordinary satirical climax, on the occasion of Bianca's coronation: "Addì dodici d' ottobre la scappata di Venezia, la doppia adultera d' un marito legittimo e di una moglie legittima(a), la stipendiatrice di un' Ebrea ribalda, l' ucciditrice di tre donne chiamate da lei a fiato parto(b) fu portata trionfalmente con la corona in testa." *t. c.* 174. One would think that where Eleonora and Isabella lent examples of royal dissoluteness, where Don Pietro sinned against nature, and Francesco (as said) retailed the poisons of his father's private shop, Bianca might have been reserved for the middle tints of the picture, nor made to bear its broadest sunlight and intensest shadow; but the

(a) One instance is not proved. For the other, nine hundred and ninety-nine women out of a thousand would in the same circumstances have done as I suppose the widow of Bonaventuri may have done, and the thousandth would have thought she was doing no harm in committing adultery with the eyes. This, in any age and any country. And Botta, if he knew mankind as he ought to have known, must have been aware of this, call it weakness, or depravity, (and it is both). Why then launch into such special vituperation against this one calumniated head? Christ would have turned round on her accusers and written in the sand.

(b) I need not repeat, where was the use of slaying them, if Bianca did not hesitate to reveal the plot? Botta here, in his love of verbal painting and epigrammatic force, forgets probability, if not ignores his own assertions.

quote it, and we may rest assured that in her relations as Grand-duchess she did nothing to lessen the devotion of her lord, a devotion which taking the archival record of his death as veritable (which I do not) was evidenced, even in the belief of his enemies, by his latest breath. *Cons.* y. 1587.

One word more. The account of Bianca's foisting a spurious off-spring on the Grand-duke is renewed, in the form of a suspicion, on every recurrence of her pregnancy. The historians endeavor to jus-tify their aspersion by her supposed sterility, a supposition which ap-pears to rest on no reasonable foundation. Bianca, to have the grace that is ascribed to her by her calumniators, must have been perfectly well-made, and was therefore fitted by nature for reproduction. She had born a daughter (Pellegrina) to her first husband. What ground was there for supposing that married to the Duke, a member of a pro-lific family, and who had had children by the feeble, stunted and pallid Joanna, she should suddenly lose fecundity? *v.* under yy. 1586, 1587. Galluzzi, we have seen, says she had become sterile through the use of medicines and by dissipation ; and Botta repeats, with an addition, — " Per medecine, per disordini, per corrutela." These assertions must be, at the strongest, conjectural ; but what do they mean ? There is, I repeat, no one charge, no suggestion even of incontinence on her part, not a word said of intemperance : and merely high-living would not produce sterility, nor would obesity, unless it were natural and not the result (if it ever be) of intemperate living. Are such vague charges to be admitted without one syllable of proof? and of all the contemporary writers, edited and unedited, is there none to back these attestations with a single instance ? Let them then be dis-missed as the malice of her arch-enemy and the inconsiderate abuse of those who are not her friends. To prove Bianca sterile there was a powerful motive ; to assert that she was so is not to prove it. This

spirit of the dead Cardinal hovered over the name he had made infamous and sought to obliterate, and added his immortal hatred to the sarcasm of a pen cruel at times as the poison, the halter, or the knife, of the writer's hated Medici.

talk of sterility caused in a married woman of thirty by her dissipation may do for the 16th century, but will not for this.(17) If Bianca, after producing Pellegrina, really was incapable of bearing more children, it was the defect of her organization and had nothing to do with her course of life. But the probability is, that that vile poisoner, the second son of the poisoner Cosmo, was only at his father's practices. What were the colic spasms which took off, once before, his brother's hope of issue by Bianca? It may have been even that the premature delivery of Joanna (see y. 1578) was some of his doing.(18) He knew not then that his brother would wed Bianca ; and it is certain that his rage at that disappointment of his hopes was greater than was decent. See, as before, yy. 1586, 7. These terms "disordini," "coruttela," "medicine," were, I little doubt, invented by the Cardinal or his partisans to substantiate the accusation of the plot, and to justify the assertion that her various pregnancies were simulated.

Finally, the Duke, who, according to Botta, knew that this was a supposititious child, recommends him, according to Galluzzi, to the care of the Cardinal, and the Cardinal Grand-duke, as I have twice implied and as will be seen presently, takes care of him, and suffers him to enjoy the name he thought too good to be defiled by a child of the Senator Capello ! In fact, the whole thing is an absurd jumble. I believe the facts are just as I have given them in the play. If that be romance, never did romance in my opinion come so near to history, as surely in this episode of the House of Medici never did history borrow so much from romance.

Joanna died the 11th of April, 1578, — "attraversatosi il feto già 1578 *morto* nell' utero," —not having strength to sustain the remedies of art. (*Granduc.* ii. 299.) This was nearly two years *after* the deaths of Isabella and Eleonora. Noble, whom for obvious reasons I have followed in the text, says she died April 6, 1578, in premature

(17) Witness the present Queen of Spain.

(18) I am speaking with due reflection, when I say I do not believe the Cardinal was in anywise too good to have abused his intimacy for that purpose.

· labor, shocked by the murder of Isabella and Eleonora, who were both
strangled on the same day. Galluzzi would have it that the honors
paid to Vittorio (Bianca's brother) on coming to Florence contributed
to Joanna's death.(19)

. . " Era [Joanna] di piccola statura, di faccia pallida, e di aspetto
non vago." (ib. p. 299.) The Cardinal a great favorite of Joanna's.
[We may suppose him therefore fomenting the dissatisfaction of the
people, who, we are told, libeled the Duke while they praised the
Duchess.] This period was the epoch of the fiercest discord between
the brothers, "non più velata dalla dissimulazione ma ratificata al
pubblico da molte apparenti dimostrazioni." (ib. 300.)

Antonio e Piero Capponi and Bernardo Girolami, the most distinguished of the rebels who had acted with Pucci and Ridolfi, fled to
France, where they openly defamed Francesco. And the Cardinal
maintained constant relations with that country. (ib.) Here too Galluzzi shows a spirit of animosity to Francesco ; for he says that the
desire of vengeance, "passione predominante nelli spiriti deboli," [a
false assumption and contradicted by his own example, not to say of
the Cardinal, yet of Cosmo, whose mind was anything but a weak one]
animated him to put an end to the chief conspirators there. [Yet he had
endeavored to disarm Orazio Pucci by numerous benefits, and it was the
Cardinal who suggested the arrest of this hereditary rebel.] Curzio
Picchena da Colle was Secretary of the Embassy, a young and enterpris-
ing man. He was provided with poison, etc. Forty thousand ducats
promised for each death, *besides expenses !* (ib. 301.) This too Sismondi, who adds : "Il lui [le G.-d. à Picchena] fit passer des poisons
subtils, dont Cosme 1er *avait établi dans son palais une manufacture,*

(19) We are reminded of the avowal or boast, — "all extracted faithfully from
the Medicean Archives." The singleness of his sources of information tends to
render Galluzzi's volumes unreliable as a history.

It will be elsewhere seen, that a modern writer has found in the same Archives
evidence sufficient to overthrow *all*, and absolutely, the opinions previously
formed as to the character of that abominable woman, Caterina de' Medici ! They
must be, as he says, *a precious deposit of historical documents !*

qu'il prétendait être un atelier de chimie pour les expériences " ; and so on, after Galluzzi. *Répub. Ital.* t. 10. p. 226 *sq.* — Girolami died, and the rest [mark this !] lay the murder on the Duke ; of whose criminality Galluzzi adduces no one proof. They, the conspirators, dispersed themselves in France and England ; but the cut-throats of the Grand-duke followed them and "in course of time gave him all the satisfaction he desired."(2)) A Florentine assassin, broken on the

(20) We have seen how Botta speaks of Francis, — *the stupid and cruel Medici.* Sismondi's summing-up of his character is as follows : "François, tout aussi perfide, tout aussi cruel, que son père, mais bien plus dissolu(a), bien plus vaniteux,

(a) Than Cosmo ! who was said, on more than suspicion, to have debauched both his own daughter and the betrothed of his son. Where are the victims of Francesco's lust ? We hear of none but Bianca, who is reproached with having made him hers ! And for her his passion, which in 1576 had already lasted thirteen years, showed no abatement. This in itself is inconsistent with the charge of dissoluteness, which supposes indulgence in various amours, and cannot apply to one attachment, whether sanctioned by the Church or not.

In note (11) I quoted largely from a special chapter of Galluzzi's showing that in the particulars that made Cosmo's reign illustrious Francesco's was not less splendid than his.* We are told there, besides, that the former spent whole days in the galleries of his art-collections. With such a record, he could not have been dissolute were he married to half a dozen Biancas and enamored of them all. In dissoluteness men gives up his brain. The abuse of those life-energies which God designed, as with other animals, but for the reproduction of the kind, is incompatible with continued study and such application to the interest of the arts and of learning as we have seen ascribed, with compulsory truth, to the G. Duke Francis.

In every drawing of an historical character, consideration should be had to the manners of the time. We shall presently see what were the morality and decency of the Court of Catharine of Medici. The Bassompierre incidentally mentioned in a previous passage, who bridges over for us in this relation the end of the 16th and the beginning of the 17th century, is an evidence that the profligacy of persons of rank in the era I am busy with was not evanescent either in its grossness or its excessive turpitude. That favorite of Henry IV., and ornament of the Court of Louis XIII., confessed to a ruffianly complicity in the most brutal of all outrages ; an act for which he ran so nearly being stoned, as he deserved to be fully, by the people of the place of the occurrence.† This was in 1601, seventeen years after the death of Francesco, who is handled by historians as if he were the only sinner, where in his position there were was scarcely any other class. So with his alleged cruelty : it was the characteristic of the age. Henry III. of France, a prince who, though debauched by the devilish artifices of a bad mother — a Medici, was not without virtues, got rid of two dangerous enemies, the Duke and the Cardinal of Guise, by assassination. This was in 1588. In 1589, he was himself murdered.‡ In 1584, William of Orange underwent the same fate in the Netherlands. Not thirty years before (1555-6) occurred in England the burning of the heretic bishops and other reforming clergy, while Scotland was defiled in 1547 by the murder of Cardinal Beaton, of Rizzio in 1566 and of Darnley in 1567. In 1572 took place the massacre of the

* I am not claiming for it beneficence, nor wisdom. The money bestowed in collecting, at extravagant prices, treasures of ancient art in statuary and in medals alone, should have been rather devoted to his people's solid advantages. But neither was Cosmo in the least degree beneficent ; and compared with his reign who bears the epithet of *Great*, in what is Francis' less honorably conspicuous, even by Galluzzi's own acknowledgment ? The strong animal blood of the Medici was as productive of vices and of crimes (taking the record at the worst) in one as in the other.
† Happily, the villany designed was not consummated, although the outrage was. See his own Memoirs, ap. Petitot, t. XIX. (Paris 1822) p. 323. As he was rewarded for his vile complaisance by an honor that gratified his vanity as a courtier, we may suppose that his compunction — ("*ce que je fis a grand regret, et ces pauvres filles pleuraient*" —) was stifled by one of the meanest of motives.
‡ To the great joy of his Catholic subjects, and of the Pope, Sixtus V., who " feared not to sanction in cold blood, in full consistory, the regicide . . and elevating the name of James Clement above those of Judith and Eleazar Maccabeus, compared the miraculous event to the Incarnation and the Resurrection of the Lord " ! MARTIN (after De Thou) : *Hist. de France,* ed. c., t. xi. p. 210, note.

wheel, confessed to having been sent expressly into France by the G. D. to murder Troilo Orsini [one would have thought the D. of Bracciano had been the more likely instigator] for six thousand ducats, and after-

bien plus irascible que lui [how does this accord with his dissimulation, as Galluzzi states it?], *n'avait aucun des talents par lesques Cosme 1er avait fondé sa grandeur* [it was something more than *talents* Cosimo employed]. Aussi fut il, plus encore que lui. l'objet de la haine des peuples. et cette haine n'était mêlée *d'aucun sentiment de respect pour son habileté*." *R. It. t.* 10. p. 225. Galluzzi, inconsistent with himself, writes in positive contradiction to all the chief points in this repulsive picture. After saying he w s the greatest dissembler of all princes, inexorable with his inferiors. and with his equals haughty to the degree of wishing their humiliation, he declares on the other hand, his laws show him to have been a Prince *just and impartial, an enemy of corruption*, "*amorevole con i suddetti*" [reconcile this to the "inexorable. etc." above, for I can not], *e fornito di tutte quelle qu ilit che si desi levano in un Regnante*." If he was *furnished with all those qualities which are desirable in a sovereign*, what are we to

nobles in Sweden. The atrocities of that pious hypocrite and sanguinary egotist, that superlative compound of all that is vile in the priesthood and odious in kings, Philip II. of Spain, who could not die without a fourteen-times-repeated sacrament, the atrocities perpetrated or sanctioned by him everywhere where his power extended, from the privacy of his palace to the utmost reach of his wide dominion (1556-159e), are familiar to the history-classes of every school. And in 1572 took place the Massacre of St. Barthelomew, when the groans of thousands of butchered heretics made music to the ears of Satan, and echoed so delightful to the fancy of Gregory XIII , that, not content with celebrating the glorious event by cannon-firing, illuminations and a solemn procession to the churches of a God of Peace, he had a medal struck, in which the Destroying Angel on one side was balanced by his own bust on the other. — Everywhere blood, blood; and blood shed tyrannically, barbarously, basely. But centuries make no difference in the record of human crime. Two hundred and ninety years after the infernal blood-bath of St Barth lomew, a traitorous part of the low Irish in this city enacted in a narrower shambles, on inoffensive blacks, the God-defying butchery which the papistical zealots perpetrated on Coligni and his correligionists, — crushing out their brains with stones and suspending their quivering bodies to lamposts, and, with a savageness of fury that cannot be called vindictive rage, beating to death, dragging through the kennels, and hanging up his muddy, half-eviscerated and scarcely-recognizable remains, their own countryman who in his military office was man and citizen enough to adhere to his duty, — and this from no religious antipathy, but from a latent envy, mingled strangely with barbarous contempt, and roused to violence by partisan hatred of the great government that protected them and enabled them to obtain from a corrupt and semi-foreign municipality, disloyal like themselves, their absurd privileges. Two years later, after acts of atrocious inhumanity committed in cold blood by the despairing Rebels, and wanton piracies, and robbery, and schemes of disgusting villany for the conflagration of great cities and the introduction into the n of the desolation of pestilence, occurred by the hand of a political fanatic the death of President Lincoln, even such a murder as those of Henry III. and IV. of France and William of Orange. Were I to write one word as the Finis of the universal history of mankind from fabulous Adam down, — a word that should express the lesson to be gathered for man's hope of moral betterment, — it would be — DESPAIR.

* The Holy Father, who saw the necessity of reforming the Calendar for the sake of the Church, had no idea of a reformation in the Church itself. So, in addition to other signs of approbation, the arch apostle of peace and good-w ll unto men caused a picture to be made of the massacre and exhibited in the Vatican "en lieu très-apparent et honorable ", where, according to M. Martin, it stimulates devotion still. *Ib.* 597 sq.

ward retained for other murders. He said moreover that the Ambassador and Secretary had frequent interviews with him for the purpose. [All this, remember, on the assertion of a hired assassin. But it is certainly an extraordinary indication of the state of the times in which such an accusation could be made against an ambassador.] The Secretary (Picchena) in consequence was arrested. Out of friendship however for the Medici he was released, but banished perpetually. *Granduc.* ii. 325, sq. See remonstrances of the Queen of France on this murder of Troilus, etc. *ib.* p. 356. (21)

think of those aspersions upon his rule, and upon his character both as a man and a prince, which are read not only in Sismondi as above and furnish material for the gloomy etchings of Botta, but are scattered throughout his history by Galluzzi himself? *"I suoi talenti e le sue cognizioni erano certamente superiori a quelle di qualunque Principe dei suoi tempi, ec. ec." Granduc.* ii. 423. It is impossible to get over the positiveness of this declaration, which moreover is maintained by an enumeration of the accomplishments for which the historian claims this superiority of Francis-Mary in talent and in knowledge to all the Princes of his time. Those who are curious in the matter will find on consulting his second volume, *Cap. X.,* such a record of Francesco's devotion to the fine arts, to the embellishment and renown of Florence through them, his encouragement of learned men, his own acquirements in the sciences, as will not only make them marvel at Galluzzi's prejudice, but pronounce the assertion of Sismondi, that the people's hatred of Francesco was qualified by no sentiment of respect for his abilities, a monstrous misrepresentation. *v. supra* (11).

(21) This was the Queen-Mother, Catharine of Medici, whom I have alluded to as lending her aid to the worst and most indecent debaucheries that ruined what was good in Henry III.(a) A detestable woman, the chief promoter if not instigator of the Massacre of St. Bartholomew(b), whose horrors she contemplated with

(a) In all her policy, Catharine made great use of handsome women and amorous intrigue, having always about her a swarm of *brilliant and facile beauties* (the phrase is M. Martin's), who went familiarly by the facetious name of her *flying squadron* — "l'escadron volant de la Reine." M var. *Hist.* X 75.

(b) Charles was full of hesitation, and even of horror as the hour approached; but Catharine stood by his side, his evil monitor, and when argument failed roused the devil of his nature by impeaching his manhood. *Id.* (after D'Aubigné), *ib.* 370. Alberi however, a life-writer presently to be cited, maintains, not only that neither of them desired or provoked the massacre, but that both used their utmost power to moderate its excesses! *Vit.* ut inf. p. 105.

Bianca, while the Grand-duke treated the Cardinal harshly,
1580 acted with great suavity and an appearance of affection and
submissiveness. — The Cardinal wanting money, and Francesco refusing an anticipation of his revenue, Bianca procured the

perfect indifference.(c)   Daughter of Lorenzo, Duke of Urbino, and niece of
Giulio, Clement VII., even her merits, like her vices, were those of her family.
That she should remonstrate against the poisoning of Troilus could have been
only because, under the circumstances, it insulted her supremacy(d), not from
scruples of conscience ; for her hand, the Medici hand, was recognized in the sudden deaths of Jane of Navarre and Mary of Clèves, and some suspected even that
she poisoned her own son Charles IX.(c)

(c) She did something more, and the historian cites it as an evidence of the depravation of morals in her
Court : " On v.t les filles d'honneur de la reine mère, et Catherine elle-même, examiner, avec des remarques
obscènes, les corps depouillés des gentilshommes huguenots de leur connaissance." ib. 260. The example
is one rather of the horrible callousness to which the common cruelty of the age had brought even the gentler
and timid sex. As for the feminine remarks, they too are rather an illustration of the coarseness of the
time than of its licentiousness : it was depravity simply naked and shameless ; for, save in the closeness and
the adornment of its drapery, the carnal-spirit, or beast-man, is much the same in all ages.
  But that ingenuous and pleasant chronicler, Pierre de l'Estoile, in his curious but valuable medley, Journal
de Henri III. (Mem. pour servir &c., in Petitot's Collection, t. 45, p. 76,) tells us something more startling than
even this indecent cruelty. Catharine, it seems, was not at all behind certain of her noble subjects, who
availed themselves of the pretext, often false, of heresy, to put to death their own relations, in order to get
possession of their property, — what might be called a natural concomitant and consequent of such commo-
tions, wherein right and wrong are often, both by accident and by design, confounded. " En ce tems [just
after the St. Bartholomew] la bonne dame Catherine, en faveur de son mignon de Retz, qui vouloit avoir la
terre de Versailles, fit étrangler aux prisons Lomenie, Secretaire du Roy, auquel ladite terre appartenoit, et
fit mourir encore quelques autres pour recompenser ses serviteurs de confiscations."
  (d) She so avowed indeed to the G. Duke's Secretary . . . "perche il G. D. non tien conto di me, anzi con
tanto dispiacer mio e del Re ci ha fatto ammazzare sugli occhi Troilo Orsini ed altri, che non ci par ben fatto,
essendo questo Regno libero, e che ognuno si puo stare." loc. cit.
  It is curious to note how the powerful animal character of the Medici is traceable even in the females. As
a rule, children take more after their mothers than their fathers, but both in Catharine and in Mary of Medici
we have the traits, not of the mother's blood but of the father's, while Charles IX. of France may be thought
to have derived his evil dispositions from his mother, as undoubtedly they were encouraged, intensified, and
brought into frightful action by that unprincipled and pitiless woman.
  (e) L'Estoile has preserved for us a rather indifferent epigram of the time on Catharine, which compares
her to Jezebel. It concludes thus :
　　　　　　" Enfin le jugement est tel :
　　　　　　　Par une vengeance divine,
　　　　　　　Les chiens mangerent Jezabel ;
　　　　　　　La charogne de Catherine
　　　　　　　Sera differente en ce point,
　　　　　　　Car les chiens n'en voudroit point." Coll. cit. t. 47. p. 80.

  Those who would see how an Italian in Florence, having at heart the honor of its once ruling family, and
writing, in this century as did Galluzzi in the last, under the auspices of a Grand-duke of the Austrian House,
and moreover an ardent Roman Catholic, has sought to explain away all the facts which have been brought
to bear against both Catharine of Medici and Charles IX., may consult Eugenio Alberi, in Vita di Caterina
de' Medici ; Firenze, in 4to. 1838. The writer says in his Preface : " Mi son trovato condotto a rovesciare
tutte le opinioni finora ricevute intorno a lei, &c." (an extensive undertaking); and paying special honor to

favor for the Cardinal, who thereupon came to Florence to show reconciliation. *ib.* 333.

The bands of predatory soldiers, who were protected secretly by the
Church-feudatories, — nay, sometimes openly assisted them, so that,
says the writer, " la depravazione facea apprendere l' assassinamento
come un esercizio cavalleresco," — added to the troubles. The most
famous of these wretches was Pietro Leoncillo da Spoleti, supposed
son of the Cardinal Farnese, who with a band of four hundred mis-
creants in various squads infested the frontiers. *ib.* 340.

1583
1584

The Cardinal dissembling "affects confidence and friendship
with the Grand-duchess." *ib.* 382.

One of the Grand-duke's favorites at this time was the Auditor
of the Treasury, Carlo Antonio del Pozzo, universally hated for his
severity in office, but of rare learning and acute intellect and aptitude
for emergencies, which compelled esteem. This office he held in
1572 —— Promoted in 1582 to the Archbishopric of Pisa —— Conducted
himself always with rectitude and disinterestedness, and, showing
gratitude to the Cardinal to whose favor he owed his first steps in good-
fortune, he used his influence with both to maintain their brotherly
unity. Such a man could not always please *the corrupt and weak*

the *Archivio Mediceo* . . " quel prezioso deposito di storici documenti " — wherein, he says, " con esito cor-
rispondente alla aspettazione, mi è venuto fatto di rinvenire gravissime ed irrefragabili testimonianze in
favore del nuovo criterio ch' io già mi era formato di Caterina de' Medici," he proceeds to assert that the
crimes imputed to her will be found not to resolve themselves into the injustice of the two factions she endeavored to conciliate, but which were emulous in her vilification.

Having myself endeavored to redeem the character of *Bianca Capello* from the calumniation of personal
enemies, I could not but look with interest upon this effort in a similar, yet in point of facts contrary,
direction. He has massed together a variety of interesting documents both as to the two chief personages
of his *Essay*, as he modestly calls it, and to characters with them historically connected intimately or re-
motely ; but he fails to overthrow, and indeed avoids attacking any one of those facts which are adduced, not
by partisan or Protestant writers, but by contemporaries and plain chroniclers who not only present internal evidence of probity, but are universally admitted to be reliable. Catharine of the Medici must, for all
the industry and patriotism of her countryman, remain a Medici, — dissolute, dissembling, intriguing, inor-
dinately as selfishly ambitious, false of tongue and frigid in heart, cruel, unscrupulous, remorseless; her
very merits, as I have elsewhere intimated, the merits of her father's family where best, — talented, adroit,
resolute, audacious, magnificent in the use of wealth, whose resources she but valued for the purposes of her
policy and the real or supposed lustre of her iniquitous administration. A bad mother, and wicked among
the wickedest of queens, she ruined body and soul two monarchs, both her sons, and has left for herself a renown indelible as that of the Massacre with which it is associated, and, since undivided, even more infamous.

Francis. — Abbioso, having now returned from Venice, because of
the rupture with that Republic, professed himself openly the enemy
of the Cardinal, to whose hostility he attributed his difficulty in getting
the Coadjutorship of the Bishopric of Pistoia at Rome, "per esser
guercio e difforme." But the new Archbishop of Pisa knew how to
preserve the esteem of all parties. Affecting [note in this sentence
the contradiction to what is said above of his constant rectitude and
disinterestedness] to make the Duke and Bianca "gli arbitri di tutte le
parti graziose del suo ministro, e mostrandosi esemplaro e zelante, si
acquistava opinione di santità e si preparava la strada al Papato."—
The Cardinal dissembling, but ill-satisfied with this position of affairs ;
—and Francesco, showing openly disregard of his dissatisfaction,
augmented the boldness of his ministers and more exasperated his
brother. (ib. 333–390.)

1585   Cardinal Ferdinand causes the election of the Cardinal Peretti
as Sixtus V., and becomes thus omnipotent with the new Pontiff.

At the marriage of Donna Virginia with Don Cesare d'Este [sub-
1586   sequently Duke of Modena], appeared her mother, the beautiful
Camilla Martelli, after a confinement of twelve years. The Cardinal and D. Pietro courted her continually and induced the chief
people of the city to honor her, in order to disgrace the Grand-duke.
p. 404. *The rumored pregnancy of the Grand-duchess induced the two
to return to Florence to watch events.* — Grand-duke shuts up again
Camilla, moved especially thereto by the secret visits of his brothers
to her. p. 405. *The brothers correspond on the reputed pregnancy of the
Grand-duchess — profess to each other suspicions that she is going to
impose a supposititious child upon the G. D., to shut them out of the succession.* p 406. D. Pietro appears throughout the dupe of the Cardinal.

The Cardinal, appearing to be reconciled, sent a gentleman, his
1587   confederate, to Florence, to announce his presence in Sep-
tember. The historian says : "Facilitò maggiormente questo ac-

comodamento l'essersi ormai assicurato [Francesco] della vanità delle
sue speranze, poichè la gravidanza della Granduchessa si era già
disciolta *con una colica e non senza grave pericolo della sua vita* [ob-
serve this !] di modo che il caso di aver prole era ormai disperato."
ib. 419. If the pregnancy was assumed, why was the deceit ended?
I should rather have suspected that the *colic*, which *put seriously
in peril her life*, was the result of poison administered through the
impulsion of one whose interest was involved in the *vanity of the
Duke's hopes*.

The Cardinal arrives October 1 —— Received with every mark of
affection and cordiality —— Went immediately with his brother and
the Grand-duchess to Villa del Poggio at Caiano — where it was customary to resort for the chase every autumn —— *Grand-duchess exerts
herself to make a sincere union between the two brothers* —— On the 5th
October, Grand-duke attacked with fever, which the physicians pronounced to be tertian —— Two days after, the Grand-duchess with the
same. — Besides the Court-physicians, Baldini and Cappelli, the Cardinal's physician, Giulio Cini, rendered his assistance. They kept the
malady concealed at first, but nevertheless confused rumors got abroad.
It was reported to the Pope, the Grand-duke had made himself sick
with eating mushrooms. But on the 16th October, it was written, *he
had a continual fever and excessive thirst*. (*ib.* 423.) On the ninth
day, the fever increased, and death ensued, October 19th. "Volle
sempre medicarsi a suo modo con cibi e bevande gelate [the desire
for *food* would be caused by the gnawing pain in his stomach, and for
the *iced drinks*, why not ?], e siccome nel corso della malattia dimos-
trò *una sete ardentissima*, fu creduto che morisse arso dai cibi e bevande
calide delle quali faceva uso assai smoderato."(22) When he knew

(22) I suppose this case of Bianca and the Grand-duke, as well as that of the
Cardinal Ippolito, to be one of poisoning by arsenic (*see* Taylor as before
cited, chap. xxiii. p. 252 sqq). According to that English toxicologist, arsenic,
though it irritates and inflames, has no chemical or corrosive action on the viscera,
although on p. 255 one doubtful instance is recorded of a seriously corrosive ac-

the malady was mortal, he called his brother, demanded pardon for the past, communicated to him the countersigns of the fortresses, recommended his spouse, Don Antonio, his ministers, and all who were

tion, the effects corresponding to that in the visceral membrane of the Cardinal. But Orfila, a much higher authority, ascribes a destructive action to irritant poisons: *Œuv. cit.* T. I. p. 75; also 421. He considers it incontestably proved, "que les plaques gangréneuses des téguments *peuvent également appartenir à tous les poisons qui agissent avec une très-grande activité." ib.* 676. This is the language, not only of experience, but of common sense. Yet while he cites (p. 76 t. l.) a case in point from Hoffman (cf. *ib.* H. 806), he quotes on p. 421 the observation of Brodie, that spots of congested blood are often taken for eschars, and instances from the same eminent English surgeon (in *Philos. Trans.* for 1812) a case where a woman dying on the fourth day, "à l'ouverture du cadavre on trouva la membrane muqueuse de l'estomac et des intestins ulcéré dans une très-grande étendue" (484 sq.). He gives moreover (with which I will conclude my ample, but I hope not uninteresting, accumulation of instances) the case from Etmüller of a young girl poisoned by arsenious acid, "*neither whose stomach nor entrails offered any trace of inflammation or of gangrene; nevertheless arsenic was found in that viscus.*" I. p. 420. Comp. ii. 895.

See *ib.* in vol. ii. p. 904 sqq., for a consideration of maladies which may be confounded with acute poisoning. The passage affords nothing to abate suspicion in the case of the Duke and Bianca, and, whether the account of their ten and eleven days' suffering be correct, or the popular one of almost immediate dissolution, there can be no doubt that the ill-fated pair were poisoned(a), while there is every probability that it was effected by arsenious acid.(b)　Galluzzi says, " Nella sezione del suo cadavere [del G. D. *sc.*] la sede principal del male apparve nel fegato " (*ut supra,* 424) : *on the dissection of the Duke's body, the principal seat of the malady appeared to be in the liver.* Now, it is precisely the *liver* which, according to Taylor, is attacked by arsenic. And further I may add, that when

(a) Siamondi himself did not doubt it : . . . "empoisonné (Français), ainsi que sa femme, dans un repas de reconciliation, etc." x. p. 227, — citing, besides Galluzzi, *Anguillasi, Notizie del Poggio a Caiano,* p. 117 ; a work I have not been able to procure. Botta rejects with easy contempt the popular traditions, but does not commit himself to any opinion of his own.

(b) The mineral poisons, and the mechanical poison (so to call it) of comminuted glass, were probably the only ones in criminal use in the 16th century. In the first decade of the 17th, we observe Shakspeare writing.

　　. . " the thought whereof
Doth, like *a poisonous mineral,* gnaw my inwards."

dear to him.(23)   The Cardinal, *comforting him, sent to take possession of the fortresses, ordered the assembling of the troops*, etc. 421. (24)

they bled him (twice!) his surgeons took the best means to give effect to the poison.(c)

(23) Was this the stupid and cruel Medici, of Botta? the perfidious, merciless, dissolute and vainglorious son of Cosmo, of Sismondi? the dissembling, inexorable and arrogant Prince, of Galluzzi? A man, I well know, may be of a loving disposition and tender almost to effeminacy, yet have that contradictory quality in him, that, when roused by anger or perturbed by bodily fear, he will be in the former case ferocious, and in the latter remorselessly, no, unhesitatingly cruel. But while this absolute fact, not hypothesis, goes to confirm the unfavorable side of Francesco's character as displayed (after the manner of his day) toward his inveterate and dreaded political enemies, yet it will not explain his devotion to his friends. A man who in his dying hour has forethought for all who are dear to him, particularizing each one, who, with that magnanimity which belongs to delicate and noble souls alone, exaggerating in his own eyes his own errors and losing sight entirely of the grosser offences of others toward him, could ask forgiveness of the brother who had persistently maligned, intrigued against, as well as hated him, and insulted the woman he passionately loved, such a man was more truly Christian than those who, forgetful of charity, emblazon but his errors and magnify his crimes.

In thus speaking, it will be seen I assume the record copied by Galluzzi to be correct. But my belief, I beg leave to reiterate, is positively to the contrary. I do not credit one word of this death-bed scene.

(24) . . "Il quale *non tardò a farsi riconoscere per padrone; perciocchè*, avendo mostrato il Castellano di Livorno *alquanto di renitenza* a consegnare quella Fortezza ad un gentiluomo da lui inviato colà con contrassegno, *il fece impiccare.*" MURATORI, *ubi cit.* The haste of the Cardinal, it will be observed, is not more remarked by Muratori than by Galluzzi. It is a precious passage that, " The Cardinal, *comforting him*, sent, &c."

Now, if the Cardinal was beloved of the people (*Galluzzi*), and if Francis died

(c) " In case of arsenical poisoning, the liver . . . is generally more strongly impregnated with arsenic than the other soft organs. The proportion of absorbed arsenic found in it is, according to M. Flandin, nine *tenths of the whole quantity carried into the circulation.* Where arsenic is not found in the contents of the stomach, and death has taken place within the usual period, it may commonly be detected *in the liver.*" Taylor, p. 29. Orfila, on the contrary, who frequently condemns the opinions of Flandin, scarcely mentions the liver, if at all, among the viscera attacked. Further, he prescribes bleeding (*after vomiting*) : i. 79.

Bishop Abbioso, Bianca's daughter Pellegrina, and Ulysses Benti-voglio her son-in-law, were charged with the care of Bianca. She died on the 20th of October. (25)

to the undissembled joy and with the universal hatred of his subjects (*Sismondi*), why did the former make such haste to seize the fortresses? to seize them even before the breath was out of his brother's body? Of whom was he afraid? Was not the throne yet firmly settled? Or was there any doubt of the illegitimacy of Don Antonio, whom he had made by a most atrocious plot to be, and still makes the world believe to have been, foisted on the Grand-duke, while a modern historian, to cap the climax of absurdity, declares him to have been, *the stupid Medici*, perfectly satisfied when the Grand-duchess with a sublime effront-ery avowed the treasonous imposition? Again, if the Cardinal was persuaded by his documents, received from the judicial examination of the Bolognese Governess, and which he took care to have preserved in the Medicean Archives, that Don Antonio was but a sprout from the soil of the people, having no claim to any con-sideration other than that of an innocent victim of the venality of his mother, why did he continue the Grand-duke's benefactions to him, so immeasurably beyond his occasions even were he noble?(a) It is obvious that there must have been doubt and uneasiness in the popular mind, or where was the need to publish that *act declaratory of the nativity of D. Antonio?* And by the by, assuming the account above to be correct, that on his death-bed the Grand-duke recommended this very youth to his brother's care, how came Botta by the story that the Grand-duke knew all about his origin? Seldom does history offer us such trumpery as is comprised in the account of the rise and fall of the Grand-duchess Bianca. But the Cardinal was able to make history for himself, and I verily believe he did it.

(25) In the second month of this same year, Mary of Scotland was murdered in another way. The coincidence is worth noting. Both nearly of an age, but Mary a little the older(b); both handsome, and with a fascination of manner that enhanced the beauty from which chiefly it was derived; both amiable, yet not

(a) "A Don Antonio de Medici conservò il trattamento e le onorificenze assegnateli da Francesco." *Grandus.* ii. 432.

The idea that he should have done this *out of regard, not only to his brother's memory, but to the innocent boy* whose more than bastardy he was proclaiming in his very face, is preposterous. D. Antonio was prob-ably as legitimate as Elizabeth of England, who too was the product of a secret marriage, and, moreover, by an act of bigamy.

(b) Bianca fled from Venice in 1563. If she was then eighteen, she was forty-two years old when poisoned. Mary, born Dec. 8, 1512, on February 18, 1587, when she was beheaded, was but a little over forty-four.

Taking this account to be accurate, we have these remarkable facts, that two persons, husband and wife, were seized with intermittent fever within two days of each other, and that, in despite of the resources of art, — for we are not told that the Duke prescribed for Bianca "a suo modo", — died within a day of each other, conveniently to make the Cardinal sovereign. It were easier to believe the murderer himself, who said (as imputed to him), that Bianca, having tried to get rid of him, had the remarkable stupidity to poison the very dish her husband was sure to eat of, and of which she herself was known to be fond, and that unable, without exciting suspicion, to prevent the Duke's indulging his appetite, herself, in her desperation and dis-

without pride and spirit; both intellectual, and one accomplished; the lives of both romantic, but one (Mary) knowing little else than misfortune, the other fortunate until her death; both calumniated, but Bianca having added to her imputed crimes the sin of witchcraft, the latter charge being reversed in Mary's case, for it was her husband who confessed he tried its futile practices upon her, while Bianca employed it, according to the Archives, on her husband, and (wonderful to relate!) with her husband's perfect knowledge. And (may I add without presumption), as in the case of *Mary Stuart*(a), so some future tragic poet may reverse the picture of *Bianca Capello*, and paint her, not such as the Grand-duke loved her, but as the Cardinal hated. The change would be still easier than with Mary, and the tragedy would be more effective. But the poet would pervert, not history, but that truth which lies often hidden in the midst of history and is only to be found by those who independently seek it out for themselves.

(a) I understand that Mr. Swinburne, in his drama of *Chastelard*, has adopted, and with earnestness, the popular view against her. It would be difficult perhaps for an Englishman to do otherwise. Were I to write a tragedy on a theme which has been consecrated by the pen of Alfieri and of Schiller, I should, and with conviction, take the other side.

The greatest source of Mary's misfortunes, and of her partial guilt, or at least of errors that partook of guilt and are arraigned as such, was her light, pliant, and thus inconstant temper. If she pardoned Bothwell, it should be remembered that she forgave too the insolent, the treasonable murder of Rizzio, although in the passion of the moment she had declared she would avenge it. In fact, she was unfitted to be a queen by those very feminine qualities which would have made her loved, honored and admired in private life, precisely as Elizabeth, by the very opposite, more than respectable as a sovereign, would have been detestable as a simple matron.

The greatest real blot upon the character of the Queen of Scots is probably that which is suggested by the name of the drama above-mentioned. The vanity of Chastelard had not carried him so far in his presumption had he not misread the encouragement in Mary's eyes. And she suffered him to be sacrificed to save her reputation. In this too she was purely feminine, women who are very women feeling no more regret for those who perish by their coquetry than for the moth which singes its wings in the caudle they dress by.

appointment, had the courage to perform a kind of internal hari-kari !

As the Duke's body was ordered to be opened, it was carried on the evening of that day to Florence with private honors, met at the gate by the clergy of San Lorenzo, the German guard and a number of his courtiers, and taken to the Church. For Bianca, Serguidi [Vittorio's successor in the Cabinet] was ordered to keep the body untouched *till evening*, and then to have it opened in the presence of the daughter, her husband, and the physicians. [The torchlight would not facilitate an inspection which otherwise was not intended to be more than formal. What passed in the minds of the daughter and husband, if not of the physicians, may be conjectured.] It was carried in the same way as the Duke's to Florence on the 21st, then buried in the vaults of S. Lorenzo, *in such a way as not to leave any memory of her:* " non volle il Cardinal Granduca che si ammettesse fra i sepolcri dei Medici, ma lo fece seppellire nei sotterranei di S. Lorenzo in modo tale che al pubblico non restasse di lei veruna memoria." *ib.* 420. Was either Isabella or Eleonora buried in the public vaults? Yet both were notoriously guilty of many adulteries, for which finally they died, and one of them besides was said to have committed incest with her own father, and the other to have gone to her virgin nuptial-bed already pregnant by her father-in-law. Bianca did not *lend an ear to every one who ogled her*, nor indulged in mean amours with her husband's pages. Yet History passes lightly over those godly actions of the princesses, or touches them with a pencil which has no caricature or a pen which writes no syllable of reproach, while for Bianca there is no abusive name too foul. Historian vies with historian to redouble epithets of contumely and to charge the picture of her imputed misdemeanors with the exaggerated traits of sarcasm. Why is this? Because, like Mary of Scots, she had personal enemies,(26) and the

(26) As the Cardinal, her lord's brother, was her adversary, at whose instigation and by whose machinations, aided often by the money he had solicited and obtained (O the meanness! and O the perfidy!) through her aid, came all the evil

archives of her husband's family have passed through fingers which
had the power to subtract and multiply at will.

Implacable in his vindictive hate, the quarterings of Bianca's arms
were removed by order of the Cardinal Grand-duke, and for them sub-
stituted those of Joanna. He could not bear to hear her even called
Grand-duchess. "Egli, irritato di tanti artifici ed intrighi di quella
donna, *non potè contenersi più lungamente nella simulazione.* Ordinò
pertanto estinguersi ogni memoria che esistesse al pubblico della sua
persona, e che si togliessero dai luoghi pubblici le di lei armi inquar-
tate con quelle de Medici con sostituirvi quelle di Giovanna d' Austria.
In progresso nel doversi far menzione di lei, *non potè soffrire che li
si attribuisse il titolo di Granduchessa,* ed egli stesso in un atto de-
claratorio dei natali di D. Antonio volle che si denominasse replicata-
mente *la pessima Bianca."* 425, 6.

The historian goes on then to relate what he calls the *imaginary* accounts. Bianca wanted to poison the Cardinal by a tart. The Cardinal had a ring which changed color, and warned him. He would not
partake of the tart. Francis, not aware of the danger, ate of it, and

---

that accompanied her latter days and survived her in an infamous renown, so it
was the natural brother of Queen Mary (Earl of Murray) who was the secret instigator and promoter of all the schemes of her Protestant enemies. Muratori,
ad ann. 1587, records the tragical result in this manner: — " L'anno fu poi questo,
in cui Elisabetta, Regina Eretica d' Inghilterra, con eterna sua infamia, condannò
alla morte Maria, Regina Cattolica di Scozia, non suddita sua, dopo la prigionia di
moltissimi anni. *Fu ella e prima e dipoi oppressa da infinite calunnie de'
suoi nemici,* per tentar pure di giustificar l' atto barbaro e tirannico d' Elisabetta,
riprovata da chiunque portava il titolo di Principe(a)." *Annal. d' Italia* (in
4to, Napoli, 1773), t. x. p. 462. Exception being made to his undissembled prejudice against the *heresiarch* Elizabeth, his remarks are just, and would apply,
mutatis mutandis, to Bianca.

(a) This is an error. It was approved, as an act of policy, (as if policy could ever sanction crime, or lend
more than the shadow of palliation to usurped power and to injustice!) by two or three, among whose
names, if my memory does not deceive me, was the honorable and ever to be honored one of Henry of
Navarre.

Bianca, fearful of the consequence, partook. *ib.* "Imaginary," so far
as this statement goes. But whence came the narrative which reverses
all this, and which Noble gives, and I have adopted in the play ?(27)
This account says, that there was served at the repast *blancmange*, of
which the Duke was extremely fond. Ferdinand would not eat of it,
pretending illness and disordered stomach. The poisoned pair were
removed, in convulsions, to the only gloomy apartment in the whole
villa. After their death, and then only, the Cardinal threw open the
doors. He pretended Bianca wished to poison him, but, seeing her
husband eat of the envenomed sweetmeat, *etc.* (as above.) Here, it
will be perceived, there is nothing in the detail that partakes of the
marvelous or appeals to popular superstition. And it is perhaps for
that reason, which adds to .ts probability, that Galluzzi avoided men-
tioning it, for it certainly was as worthy of record, even if based on
vulgar fallacy, as its fellow-tradition. But in fact, this story has a
particularity as well as plainness and naturalness of description which
will not allow us, when considering all the circumstances preceding
and following, and the ambitious and rancorous character of the Cardinal, — a dissembler even by the acknowledgment of his eulogist,
forever plotting, and as unscrupulous as untiring in his schemes of personal aggrandizement, — will not allow us, I say, to ascribe it wholly
to the ordinary invention and exaggeration of popular rumor ;
although, were it otherwise, the story, accepted by writers of that

(27) In Muratori we are tol l, the Grand-duke died of an affection ("infermità ")
supposed not to be dangerous, and Bianca *fifteen hours after.* According to a
cont. mporary, many believed that Bianca, " donna di altero spirito," poisoned
the Grand-duke ont of jealousy, and then herself; others, that the Cardinal poisoned both. *A·nal. d' It.* t. c. p. 461.

It is plain enough, that the supposition of empoisonment, whether a murder or
both murder and self-murder, was widely prevalent, if not the universal be'ief in
Florence. The circumstances of the twofold death, and of the malady preceding
it, were then such as to excite this belief or suspicion. Consequently, if we set
aside the nearly simultaneous attack an l its results, they could not have been
such as detailed in the Archives.

and subsequent times, is sufficient for the purpose of the dramatist who believes, as I do, that he does not pervert the truth and give, to the great names of history, characters, whether for good or evil, that are undeserved.

III.

Portraits of Bianca, etc.

Having alluded in the text to a picture of *Bianca* by Titian, I have thought it would interest the reader to be told of certain portraits, both of her and of the *Grand Duke*, still extant in Italy.

At the time the tragedy was written, I did not know that the immortal colorist had really given to the world a likeness of its heroine. I merely supposed so probable a fact to aid the *costume*, — that is, to invest the scene with those adventitious circumstances which lend it reality, and make a picture of Venetian life, for example, seem truly such by local *accidents*, which recall from time to time the place and era to the spectator's mind. But it appears that there is actually such a painting extant, and that it is, as I pretended, " One of the best from old Vecelli's hand." *v. infra. p.* 416, *sqq.*

In Count Litta's costly work (*Fam. Cel. Ital.*, Milano 1825, in fol.), in Vol. II., is a bust-portrait of Bianca after Bronzino (Gallery of Florence). It is in colors. The face is very full, with the golden-tinged fair hair which Titian and Giorgione loved and understood so well to paint, very regular, long and delicately-arched eyebrows, full and expanded forehead(1), eyes large and blue, and lively in expression,

(1) Too much so for beauty. This is partly owing to the manner of dressing the hair, which is reverted on all sides, but partly may arise from the bad judgment of the painter in exaggerating its surface, — as many English artists do, absurdly and untruthfully, the size of the eyes.

nose not delicate though regular, (there seems to be a defect in the
drawing, or in the copy, which has thrown it a little to one side), and
rather too large in the nostrils, lips curved and in proportion, but not
handsome, and with an expression not agreeable ; the contour of the
face more round than oval, — indeed of a faulty oval.   There is nothing
of the pride which Noble saw, or thought he saw, in the pictures at
Strawberry Hill, nor yet of dignity, but rather of good humor and a
slight degree of mischievousness and jocoseness.   You see from the
complexion and from the fulness and *morbidesse* of the flesh, that she
must have been a voluptuous-looking blonde, one of that kind of
women whose flesh is very white and delicate in the skin, but not firm,
with eyes of a true blue, red lips, and faultless teeth, who more than
any others have power both to waken passion and to keep it lively in
the amorous.

It is probable that this polychrome is a bad miniature of an unfaith-
ful picture ; for, as I have implied, there are faults in it which will
indicate, to any one moderately familiar with the art, that the portrait
was not true to nature, and that its faults have been exaggerated by
the copyist-designer.   It is true, the picture is of the Grand-duchess,
not of the blooming maid whom Bonaventuri, with a fortune that
makes his name seem almost the adaptation of fiction, snatched from
her native soil to transplant where at a future day she should become
the adornment of a royal garden, but even thus regarded, over expanded and partly faded, there is something *clumsy*, so to say, about
the face, which cannot be Bianca.   I am the more disposed to believe
this from the fact that in Litta's plates the engraving after Titian of
the Cardinal Ippolito in Hungarian costume differs strikingly in the
expression as well as in the eyes from the copy of the same work in
the collection known as the Pitti Gallery.(2)   Here we have the eyes

(2) *Tableaux*, etc. *de la Gall. de Florence et du Palais Pitti :* in fol. Paris
1814. *T.* III. *Tab.* 12. — This and all the works consulted in the Appendix
will be found in that Library which the far-reaching judgment and the munifi-
cence of Mr. Astor ordained to be something more than an ornament of our city.

placed at a normal distance apart ; but in the former they are so close together as to add very unpleasantly to the sharpness of the face in general, which is handsome but rather effeminate.(3)

(3) As the Cardinal is mentioned with some particularity in both the preceding Appendices, and is an interesting character in himself, especially to those who consider what might have been the fortunes of Tuscany, had he, instead of his cousin, been chosen to grace the unlawful title of Duke, with Cosmo thus shut out perhaps forever from the opportunity of an election, a description of his picture will not be amiss, although it bears but a remote connection with the text, and in an illustrative point of view is valuable solely from the light it throws upon the Romish rank of Cardinal conferred upon the younger sons of princes or the bastards of men of power, without regard to character or qualifications or age, as a provision and a probable steppingstone to the Papacy. In this same casual light we are to consider the ecclesiastical function of the Cardinal Ferdinand, who, equally unqualified, though in another way, took it up as if it were but the mantle of a dead man, when his brother, D. Giovanni, on whom it was originally bestowed, came to his untimely end.

The Cardinal Ippolito is represented with both mace and sword, and on the ugly hat or *toque*, red like the rest of the habit, is a variegated plume, the principal feather of which is green. We are told that this portrait was taken at Bologna in 1530, when Titian went thither to paint Charles V. Ippolito was then in his twentieth year, an age when foppery is pardonable in a handsome man, nor is to be repressed though you wed him to the Church. Titian at the time was in all the splendor of his power, and Vasari ranks this among the best of his portraits. The nose is delicate and rather sharp, the mouth well-formed, but, contrasted with the nose, sensuous. The expression of the eyes, as of the character of the face, is that of a generous, amiable, gentlemanly fellow, but who was not wanting in irascibility. There is no appearance of that pride which Varchi says he had in excess, neither in the style of his head nor its carriage, nor yet in the attitude, which, by the by, is without dignity, if not awkward, the habit moreover being to the last degree ungraceful.

There is another picture of Ippolito done by Pantormo. He is here in armor, and a legend tells us he was then in his eighteenth year. He looks eight and twenty, even in the beard, which may be called an impossibility in so mere a youth. It is a fine face, manly, very regular, very handsome. One hand rests on

On the same folio with *Bianca* is a portrait of the *Grand Duke* Francis, after Rubens, with an air decidedly distinguished, the face good
and regular, if not handsome. You would take the subject, if in the
ordinary costume of our own day, to be a man of consequence and of
high fashion, and somewhat of a free liver. It resembles much the
picture of Cosmo by Bronzino, in the Pitti, not merely in feature but
in the style of the head. In this latter picture, by the by, the expression of Cosmo is not what one would have anticipated from his character, but is positively good, as well as amiable, and highly intellectual.

Another bust-portrait of Francis, by Bronzino, is in the Pitti Gallery. The head large and intellectual, with great breadth and height
of forehead; eyes somewhat stern; lips well-formed and full, and
perhaps sensual; nose, good; the face oval.

In the same Gallery again (I speak of course of the engraved collection) is a portrait which is only supposed to be that of Bianca
Capello. This also is by Bronzino. There is the same want of oval in
the face as mars the one given by Count Litta; the forehead is very
high, but not so broad, nor are the eyebrows so long. The nose is
heavy, but regular, the mouth well-formed. The style of the face cor-
responds to what I have ascribed to the other. In the explanation of
the Plate (29th of the Gallery : *T.m.*), we are told: "Nous avons un autre
portrait de Blanche par le *Titien*, qui est très-différent de celui-ci, et la
gravure, due au burin de F. Clerici, en a été publiée par A. Locatelli, édi-
teur de *l'Iconographie Italienne des hommes et des femmes illustres*.(4)

his helmet, the other on his favorite dog. This is the picture that best reminds me
of Varchi's repeated eulogies; but, considering Titian's mastery in portraiture,
this, which differs widely from his, may be supposed to be no true likeness.

(4) After my death, when my countrymen may condescend to read these dramas,
I hope that some one interested in their publication will procure this work of Locatelli's, and, if the picture be as fine as represented, which may be supposed, being
by Titian and of a woman, cause a careful copy to be taken for the play. I should
do this now myself, and make the copy with my own hand, but my limited means

Le Titien l'a représentée dans toute sa beauté ; beauté que Botta hésite à appeler angélique ou diabolique. Tout indique que ce portrait fut fait par le Titien encore jeune, car on sait qu'à ses débuts il soignait extrêmement ses ouvrages. Il n'avait pas encore acquis cette habileté, cette franchise de pinceau, qui ne suffraient pas de retouche, comme on le remarque dans ses dernières productions.(5)

" Ce que nous disons vient à l'appui de l'opinion de ceux qui pensent que c'est là la Blanche Cappello de Bronzino, quoique les deux portraits n'aient presque pas de ressemblance entre eux.(6) Titien

are exhausted in the manufacture of these volumes, for which I have difficulty in finding, not readers merely, but even a publisher.

(5) This is a positive error, and a very curious one. Titian was born in 1477, and died, as the writer himself says, in 1576, being then in his hundreth year. Bianca, we have seen, left Venice in 1563; consequently, when Titian was eighty-six years old. If painted two years before her flight, when we may suppose her to have been at most sixteen, he was then eighty-four.

The error is enhanced by what the writer says of the *retouching*, although the passage is obscure in its construction and contradictory. Titian, or I am deceived, never gave up entirely, notwithstanding his temporary change of manner, that frequent manipulation which in itself alone would distinguish his handling from that of Rubens even were not the results and the general effect so different in the two chief colorists. This punctiliousness, this going over and over again, to bring the part up or down to the tone required, and to educe that harmony which is so undefinable and yet so sensible, was in fact a part of his method, and not merely the derived habit of his school, whose master was Bellini.(a)

(6) This difference in portraits is another, though a minor one of the perplexities of history. We scarcely find two pictures of any eminent person done by different hands, that are precisely alike. Sometimes the divergence is so great that no trace of resemblance can be found between them. The likenesses of Bianca Capello, if we include even that by Titian, do not probably differ from one another so much as the two of Mary Stuart given by Albèri in his Life of Catharine

(a) It was while this play was going through the press, that news came of the destruction by fire of Titian's masterpiece, the *Peter Martyr*, a work which even Haydon, when denying ideality to the Venetian school of color, expressly excepted. It is an event that I wish, for my own satisfaction, to thus chronicle, though with a feeling of pain that will have been shared by all the artist-world.

18*

mourut en 1576, et la Duchesse en 1587. Le portrait qu'il nous en a donné indique une jeune fille de moins de vingt ans, et c'est une œuvre d'une perfection exquise. Bronzino, au contraire, nous présente cette femme célèbre déjà sur le retour. * * * Dans le tableau de Vecollio, la coiffure et le vêtement sont de Venise, tandis que les accessoires dans le portrait de Bronzino ont un caractère florentin, ce quelque chose d'espagnol qui au XVIe siècle se répandait dans toute l'Italie."(7)

It is easy to see, even from this evidently defective portrait of Bianca on the wane, that she must have been, in the high day of her attractions, as I judged by the picture in Litta's plates, one of those blondes, whose flesh is rather soft than firm, but exquisitely fine of surface, and in which the red and white, red of the brightest and white of the purest, are so commingled, without the skin's appearing

of Medici. The one from the Orleans Gallery is fat, voluptuous, heavy in the nose, bad in the mouth ; and we should have to look long to find out a point of similarity between the picture of Catharine hers lf (when Regent), as given from the Florentine Gallery, and the very attractive one, as Queen, which precedes the title and is after Allori.

The portrait of a beautiful woman will be more or less beautiful, according to the circumstances, with herself and with the painter, under which it was taken. That, which at one time and with a certain pencil comes out embellished, is at another time and by another hand di-figured. The sun himself, or his apprentices, distort, and everybody knows how photographs may libel. It must be accepted that when History is single-voiced in attesting to the charms of any noted personage, and the effects ascribed to them corroborate the testimony, that picture, which, with all allowance made for the anticipation of the imagination, so certain to prepare for us disappointment, is positively ugly, or without attractiveness, has been itself a failure, not the subject of it over-drawn.

(7) He need not have confined it to Italy. It was the court-fashion of the time. We see the high and ample ruff in the portraits of Mary of Scots and of Elizabeth of England. In the one of the former that is particularized in the previous note, it is of the most preposterous description and as it were a caricature of the fashion in the supposed *Bianca* of Bronzino.

mottled, that it is difficult to say where one begins and the other ends. The fairness as well as fulness of the flesh is especially conspicuous in the neck, in the hinder part of which, and behind the ears, the white grows captivating. Eyes of the deepest blue, large, tender or lively, according to the will or the emotions of the owner ; light, but very long lashes ; brows regularly arched, very distinct, and of a rather deeper brown than the hair, which latter sparkles in the sunshine like threads of gold, is so fine as to be taken up by the lightest air, yet so thick as to show deep shadows ; nose regular, but too fleshy to be delicate ; a mouth well formed, — of a red, deep rather than bright, and dry, — the lips full and voluptuous without being sensual ; the chin round and fleshy, and, with the lobes of the ears, looking as if tempting to be pinched or pressed. Add to this, the charm of harmony and softness yet brightness of colors, those *manifold attractions* which all the writers speak of and Botta seems to grow enamored of, and which come not only of beauty but of mind, and of the heart, which latter lends the Christian grace of gentleness and winning amiability, and we have before us that Venetian, who the Cardinal taught Florence to believe was subtle and perfidious, and whom Botta, without questioning the suspicious Archives, or following Galluzzi implicitly, knew not whether to pronounce *angelical* or *of the devil.*

END OF THE FIRST VOLUME.

www.ingramcontent.com/pod-product-compliance
Lightning Source LLC
Chambersburg PA
CBHW030123030726
47498CB00007B/2522